"I Will Not Sleep With You, Lyon,"

Elizabeth said.

"You agreed," Lyon said softly.

She fought against a shiver of awareness. He was standing close behind her, his warm breath caressing the back of her head, his scent teasing her senses. "I agreed to come live with you, to stay with my son," she told him. "I did not agree to sleep with you."

"Elizabeth, be realistic." He raised a hand to her shoulders.

"No, don't." She shrank back. "Don't touch me."

She swiped at the tears streaming down her face.

"I will not listen to any more of your threats. I'll stay here, because you've given me no choice. But I won't cater to your every whim. And I absolutely won't sleep with you." She drew herself up proudly. "You can take it or leave it. Or you can go to hell."

Dear Reader,

Happy New Year! And what a *fabulous* year it's going to be. First, due to *overwhelming* popular demand, we have another fun-filled lineup of *Man of the Month* books . . . starting with *Lyon's Cub* by Joan Hohl. In the future, look for *Man of the Month* stories by some of your favorite authors, including Diana Palmer, Ann Major, Annette Broadrick and Dixie Browning.

But Silhouette Desire is not only just *Man of the Month,* because each and every month we bring you six sensuous, scintillating, love stories by six terrific writers. In January, we have Jackie Merritt, Amanda Stevens (this is her long-awaited sequel to *Love is a Stranger* and it's called *Angels Don't Cry*), Kelly Jamison, Cathie Linz and Shawna Delacorte.

And in February we're presenting a special promotion just in time for Valentine's Day called *Mystery Mates*. Read and see how each Bachelorette opens the door to love and meets the Bachelor of her dreams. This promotion is so wonderful, we decided to give you six portraits of the heroes, so you can see each man up close and *very* personal.

Believe it or not, that's just what I have in store for you the first *two months* of 1993—there's so much more to come! So keep reading, enjoying and letting me know how you feel.

All the best,

Lucia Macro
Senior Editor

JOAN HOHL

LYON'S CUB

SILHOUETTE *Desire*

Published by Silhouette Books New York

America's Publisher of Contemporary Romance

SILHOUETTE BOOKS
300 East 42nd St., New York, N.Y. 10017

LYON'S CUB

Copyright © 1993 by Joan Hohl

ISBN: 0-373-05762-8

First Silhouette Books printing January 1993

Printed in the U.S.A.

Books by Joan Hohl

Silhouette Desire

A Much Needed Holiday #247
Texas Gold #294
California Copper #312
Nevada Silver #330
Lady Ice #354
One Tough Hombre #372
Falcon's Flight #390
The Gentleman Insists #475
Christmas Stranger #540
Handsome Devil #612
Convenient Husband #732
Lyon's Cub #762

*Desire trilogy

Silhouette Romance

A Taste for Rich Things #334
Someone Waiting #358
The Scent of Lilacs #376

Silhouette Special Edition

Thorne's Way #54
Forever Spring #444
Thorne's Wife #537

Silhouette Books

Silhouette Summer Sizzlers 1988
"Grand Illusion"

Silhouette Intimate Moments

Moments Harsh, Moments Gentle #35

JOAN HOHL,

a Gemini and inveterate daydreamer, says she always has her head in the clouds. An avid reader all her life, she discovered romances about ten years ago. "And as soon as I read one," she confesses, "I was hooked." Now an extremely prolific author, she is thrilled to be getting paid for doing exactly what she loves best.

For my niece
Tracy Reitenauer:
Our family's own Second Officer,
flying for United Airlines.
I'm proud of you, Kid.

And for
Melissa Senate:
My new editor at Silhouette.
Welcome to my slightly offbeat world, Mel!

One

She was more beautiful than he remembered.

His stare riveted on the young woman, Lyon Cantrell stepped back into the deep shade of the canopied doorway of the Elegant Man clothing emporium.

Lyon wasn't aware of the disgruntled glance aimed at him by a frowning customer brushing by to enter the shop, or even the white-knuckled grip he had on the distinctive silver and black striped store bag he was clutching in his right hand.

Every molecule of Lyon's awareness was centered on the woman standing next to—actually propped against—a parking meter outside the barber shop, three stores down the street from the Elegant Man.

The years had been kind to Elizabeth Ware—more than kind. There were changes in her appearance, of course. Ten years' worth of changes. But, from his vantage point, Lyon could see that those changes were all to Elizabeth's advantage.

She had always been beautiful; now, at what? Twenty-seven? Lyon gave a brief shake of his tawny head. She was twenty-eight . . . and stunning.

Her brown hair, the deep rich shade of dark chocolate, was long, below shoulder length. The naturally curly lustrous strands were unfettered, wisps blowing free in the warm summer breeze. And even from the shadowed distance, Lyon could see the sheen of health radiating from her creamy, flawless complexion. Though he couldn't see her eyes, he had perfect memory of them, the soft, dark brown he had always likened to a velvety pansy.

As her beauty, Elizabeth's figure had improved with time—and her figure had been spectacular at the age of eighteen.

Her breasts were not large, but not small, either. High and rounded, her tip-tilted breasts had been and still were an aching allure to Lyon's suddenly itching palms and dry, empty mouth.

Her waist was small, ridiculously small, drawing attention to the gentle flare of her hips and the delta of her womanhood above her impossibly long, slender legs—legs he had always secretly thought of as the weapons of a temptress.

Today those legs were encased in skin-tight, stone-washed jeans. Her breasts pushed forward against the soft knit of a brazen red T-shirt emblazoned with the logo of Mid-Continental Airlines. Her slim feet were thrust into sandals comprised of three narrow strips of leather. A large leather bag was hooked over one shoulder. Oversized tortoiseshell-framed sunglasses perched on her delicate nose.

A painful tightness contracted Lyon's chest and parts below the equator belt line. Unconcerned with the pedestrian traffic, he stood, as still and formidable as the mountains looming over the small valley town of Cantrell, Pennsylvania, staring at the woman leaning against the parking meter, slanting periodic, impatient-looking glances at the big, round, serviceable watch strapped around her fragile-looking wrist.

Damn her.

Ten years. Ten long years and the mere sight of her created havoc inside him.

Lyon's lips thinned into a forbidding line as his unwilling gaze dropped to Elizabeth's mouth. Ten years, and he could still taste the unique flavor of her full lips, the sweet interior of her mouth.

Bitch.

Lyon's eyes narrowed as, against his will, memory stirred, unfurled, engulfed him, tossing him back in time—ten years in time.

It was an unusually hot summer in Cantrell. Heat shimmered in waves from the pavement and softened the surface of the black-topped roads.

School was out. Laughing, chattering youngsters from grade-school age to late teens, strolled, biked and generally clogged the sidewalks and streets.

Lyon was home for a two-week vacation, his first real visit in four years, since the summer after graduating from the Wharton School of Business at the University of Pennsylvania. And, after only three days, he was bored and getting antsy.

But Lyon needed the break from the grueling schedule his father had worked out for him, putting him through the paces to learn the ins and outs of the conglomerate of businesses that made up the family holdings.

Driving himself day and night for four years, Lyon had more than learned, he had excelled. But there was a price to pay. At twenty-six, Lyon was an expert, but he was one very tired expert.

The order came from the only person with the power to overrule his father, the chairman of the board. That person was Lyon's mother. Her orders were couched in no uncertain terms—come home and rest.

Lyon came home. Two days into his visit, he was bored to distraction. Due to having attended private schools in the winter and exclusive camps in the summer, Lyon had few friends in the community of his birth. In truth, he possessed one real friend, Huntington Melton Canon, the son of his mother's dearest friend.

Hunt was expected to arrive home momentarily, which was the only reason Lyon didn't pack his things and hightail it back to his office in New York.

Lyon had hopes that his prospects for entertainment would improve when Hunt got home. Being outgoing and gregarious by nature, Hunt knew everyone in Cantrell and the surrounding area.

Lyon was languishing by the pool, trying to look interested in his mother's chatter about her many and varied charitable pursuits, when Hunt finally put in an appearance, literally bounding onto the scene.

"Lyon! You son of a—" Hunt spied the older woman and tossed her a boyish smile "—gun. How the devil are you?" He executed a half bow as he turned. "And you, Mrs. Cantrell? You're looking as young and lovely as ever." His teeth gleamed in the bright afternoon sunlight.

Margaret Cantrell had always been a pushover for Hunt's charm; she still was.

"I'm very well, thank you, Hunt." A becoming tinge of pink flushed her well-cared-for face. "And I can see it's unnecessary to ask how you are," Margaret continued, running an indulgent, maternal glance over his tall, trimly muscled form. "You are more handsome and healthy-looking than ever."

"Ah, thank you, ma'am." Hunt flashed a disarming smile. "You never disappoint. That's the real reason I keep coming back here." He slid a taunting glance at Lyon. "Not to see this workaholic of a son of yours."

Margaret chuckled.

Lyon gave him a cynical look that didn't quite conceal his amusement. "You'll never change, Hunt," he drawled, rising to grasp the other man's extended hand. "Always the silver-tongued lady-killer."

"I?" Hunt appeared shocked. "From what I've been hearing, I was under the impression that you are building a reputation with the ladies of distinction."

Margaret's chuckle smoothed into a blatant smile of smug satisfaction. "There is one in particular."

"Mother." Lyon's tone held gentle reproof.

Her crystal-blue eyes grew wide with feigned innocence. "But..." she protested, "your relationship with Leslie isn't a secret, dear."

Lyon's sapphire-blue eyes glittered with unfeigned annoyance. "It is not a relationship."

"What is it?" Hunt asked with pointed interest, grinning in delight with the obvious can of worms he'd managed to pry open. "A passing fancy?"

"Indeed not!" Margaret exclaimed. "Leslie Broadworth is not that kind of young woman."

"Oh, Mother," Lyon groaned, flicking his hand in invitation to Hunt to take his pick of the loungers and lawn chairs scattered about. "Leslie is a beautiful woman, and a charming companion, but—"

"I'm relieved to hear it," Hunt inserted, dropping gracefully into a padded chair. "Because," he went on in tones of determination, "I intend dragging you with me to a party tonight."

Lyon frowned. "A party?"

"A party?" Margaret echoed, with obvious surprise. "I didn't know one of our friends was giving a party this evening."

Hunt's lips twitched with the repression of a smile at the words "our friends," but he kept the smile contained. "They aren't. The party is being thrown by an old high school friend of mine." The explanation said it all; Hunt had attended the local high school. "It's a combination celebration."

Margaret risked frown lines. "Whatever is a 'combination celebration'?"

"I would assume it is one party given to celebrate two separate occasions," Lyon drawled, sparing a dry look for Hunt. "Correct?"

"Got it." Hunt grinned. "You always were quick on the uptake. So, what do you say?"

"Nothing." Lyon raised a skeptical eyebrow. "I have yet to hear what—"

"But what occasions are being celebrated?" Margaret asked, her bemused tone betraying her inattention to the exchange of the men.

Lyon gave his mother a tolerant smile.

Hunt again contained his laughter as he turned to Margaret. "In part, it's a going away party for my friend," he explained. "But it's also a birthday party for his younger sister."

"Then I'm out," Lyon said flatly. "I'm not going to a party for a girl I don't know."

"Oh, cut me some slack, Lyon," Hunt retorted. "You sound like an old far—" He shot another abashed look at Margaret "—man. It'll be fun." He arched his attractively winged dark eyebrows. "Have you had your nose so glued to the grindstone you've forgotten how to let loose and have fun?"

The barb hit home. Lyon had had his nose glued to the grindstone, and although he had an easy companionship and mildly satisfying sex with Leslie, he had not enjoyed a true sense of fun in years. Still . . .

"I don't know," he hedged. "The idea of being a party crasher has little appeal."

Hunt rolled his expressive, and always laughing, dark eyes. "You are getting stuffy. You're twenty-six, old son, not the reverse.'' He shrugged. ''Besides, I mentioned your name, and Chuck said to bring you along.''

''Chuck?'' Lyon mused, frowning. ''Charles Ware?''

''On target,'' Hunt confirmed.

''Charles is going away?''

''Mmm.'' Hunt nodded, both in answer and in responsive thanks for the tall glass of iced tea Margaret had poured for him from the pitcher set on the table next to her chair. He took a long swallow of the chilled drink before continuing. ''Chuck has accepted a position with his company in one of those oil rich Mideast countries. I forget which one.'' He shrugged. ''No matter. At any rate, he is scheduled to leave next week, and his family is combining a send-off with his sister's party.''

''Do I know the family?'' Margaret asked, mirroring her son's frown.

''I doubt it, Mother.''

''Mr. and Mrs. Ware are nice people, but have always kept pretty much to themselves,'' Hunt supplied. ''He's the night-shift foreman at the shoe factory and she's the admissions clerk at the hospital.''

''Oh, I see.''

The laughter in Hunt's eyes dimmed, overshadowed by an angry glitter. ''The Wares are honest, hardworking, genuinely nice people," he gently chided his hostess. "I've known them since kindergarten."

"Yes, of course," Margaret said in feather-soothing tones. She then turned her most appealing smile on her son. "Why don't you tag along with Hunt, dear?"

Lyon looked amused, if not really interested. "Am I being maneuvered?"

"Of course." Hunt laughed, his humor restored.

"Certainly," Margaret agreed, smiling with sweet indulgence. "I insist you accept Hunt's friend's invitation to the party for his imminent departure and his little sister."

The little sister was celebrating her eighteenth birthday.

At Hunt's call of greeting, Elizabeth Ware turned, smiled, and looked up at him.

Lyon was lost in the warm velvet depths of her soft brown eyes. In an instant, his slate was wiped clean of the faint etchings made by Leslie and every other woman he had ever met.

She was the birthday girl, eighteen, the age of consent, and Lyon wanted her with an immediacy that was so intense it was almost frightening.

"Beth, I want you to meet my friend, Lyon Cantrell," Hunt said in introduction, blithely unaware of the tension crackling between them.

And it was between them, not one-sided.

Lyon could see it in the startled flicker in Elizabeth's eyes; she felt and reciprocated the sudden and electric attraction.

"The Lyon Cantrell?"

Her voice was soft, every bit as velvety as her eyes. A feather-light caress of his libido.

"Afraid so." Lyon felt a shock of amazement for the even smoothness of his voice; he could barely breathe, it was a wonder he could speak at all. "Many happy returns of the day, Miss Ware," he managed to murmur, proffering the small, brightly wrapped box containing the bauble he had purchased at a jewelry store on his way to the party.

"Why, thank you." She laughed with surprised delight on discovering the fine gold bracelet inside the black velvet box.

Lyon melted. "You're quite welcome, Miss Ware."

"Miss Ware!" She slid a teasing, sidelong glance at Hunt. "I like your friend. He's polite." She held out the bracelet and her arm in a silent plea to Lyon to fasten it around her wrist.

Hunt grinned. "Unlike me?"

She grinned back at him. "Oh, I don't expect you to be polite," she said, dry-voiced, straight-faced. "You're merely Chuck's friend... Hunt, the playboy."

"Direct hit!" Hunt cried, clutching his chest. "The blade slid silently between the eighth and ninth rib." He turned to Lyon. "Am I bleeding?"

Lyon found it easy to laugh; it was the perfect expression of the sense of relief he was feeling. For a moment he had entertained the fear that he may have miscalculated, and the attraction Elizabeth was revealing was for Hunt. An odd sensation of being somehow connected to her shivered through him as he finished clasping the bracelet to her wrist. His eyes met hers.

"Not noticeably," he replied in a deceptively casual drawl...sending visual messages to Elizabeth that were anything but casual.

Her eyes flickered once again. Message received. It was also obviously received by the young woman standing slightly behind Elizabeth, an expression of amused interest on her small, pixielike face.

"Am I a fence post? Am I a tree? Am I a mere shadow of my best friend?" pixie-face inquired of the world at large, chiding Hunt for his lapse of manners in not including her in the introductions.

"Is this a game of twenty questions?" Hunt replied with feigned innocence. "Now, I ask you, would our intelligent Chuck espouse himself to a fence post? A tree? A mere shadow of his sister's best friend?" He appeared to ponder the possibility while the others watched his performance with amusement. "I think not. Ergo, it must be the beauteous bride-to-be." He turned to Lyon. "May I present to you, Chuck's fiancée and Beth's best friend . . . Jennifer Clouser."

"Is this guy weird, or what?" Jennifer said, laughing as she took Lyon's extended right hand.

"Always has been," he agreed, while silently thanking his weird friend for insisting Lyon tag along to the combination celebration.

It wasn't until much later, when the party was in full swing, that Lyon managed a few precious seconds of semiprivate conversation with Elizabeth.

"May I see you sometime . . . soon?"

"Are you asking for a date . . . or an assignation?"

"Yes."

Her smile was faint, but loaded with intuitive feminine understanding. "When?"

"Tomorrow night?"

"What time?"

"Around nine?"

"Where?"

"Could I stop by, pick you up?" Lyon held his breath as she hesitated, considering.

"At the end of the driveway," she murmured, darting a glance around her for potential listeners. "I'll wait by the side of the road."

She was gone with a swish and swirl of her wide, ankle-length skirt.

Lyon began breathing again.

* * *

It was a balmy summer night. The moon was bright, nearly full. He parked the car off the road near the recreational lake a few miles outside of town, in the shadows beneath the concealing branches of a broad-leaved tree.

Lyon felt like a teenager. He was hot, hard, more aroused than at any time since he was a teenager. His heart thumped inside his tight chest. His palms were damp. Every muscle in his body was taut, ready for action.

Elizabeth sighed and settled her head against the padded headrest. "It's nice here."

"Yes." Lyon shifted around to look at her and felt the bottom drop out of his stomach.

Silvery moonlight played over her face and sank into the depths of the eyes she turned on him. Beyond thinking, reasoning, motivated by sheer instinct, Lyon slid across the Cadillac's bench seat to her side.

Touching his mouth to hers instilled a feeling of homecoming inside him.

Elizabeth accepted his mouth with parted lips moistened with the quick skimming of her tongue.

Groaning his need, Lyon took her mouth, and her tongue, and made them his own.

The progression was mutually spontaneous; slow, natural, and right.

He kissed her in every way he knew of and with all the expertise he had garnered in the past few years of his twenty-six years on earth.

He kissed her…soft and slow, fast and hard. Deep. Deeper. His tongue charted the sweet, wet terrain of her mouth, inviting her to explore the hot and hungry interior of his.

The first tentative probe of her tongue inside his mouth sent a searing shock from his throat to his manhood. His body throbbing a demand for more, he sought her breasts with his hands and his lips, bringing their tips into stone-hard points through the soft cotton of her blouse and the filmy nylon of her bra.

Elizabeth made a sound low in her throat, and arched her back in a silent plea for more.

Lyon's breathing was rough and uneven, but his hands were gentle and steady. Within moments both blouse and bra were smoothed from her silky torso, forgotten the instant they were cast aside.

The feel of her against his palms, his mouth, set him on fire. Murmuring his needs, desires and wants to her in terms erotic and outrageous, Lyon worshipped her with his hands and lips and tongue from the top of her head to the waistband of her skirt.

"May I?" He slid his fingers under the waistband and tugged at the barrier. "Let me, please."

Elizabeth complied at once, raising her hips to give him access to the button closure, and the freedom to glide the skirt and scrap of panties down the satiny length of her long legs.

Lyon's own confining clothes were discarded in a few quick, impatient tugs. His big hands curled around her tiny waist. Guiding her, he drew Elizabeth up and over him. A harsh groan tore from his throat as her smooth inner thighs slid along the hair-roughened surface of his own.

Gripping her waist, holding the downy delta of her body mere inches from the straining steel of his masculinity, Lyon paused, trembling.

"Are you sure, Elizabeth?" His voice betrayed the tension riddling his body. "Do you want this?"

A tremor quaked through her, felt by him where their thighs pressed together. Her voice was thin, barely audible, but certain.

"Yes, I want it. I want you."

Slowly, savoring every nuance of the moment, Lyon lowered her until his manhood nudged against the gate of her womanhood, seeking permission to enter.

Elizabeth decided the issue. Grasping his shoulders, she sank onto his lap, encasing him within the moist heat of her passion.

Lyon was immediately struck by simultaneous reactions. His body thrilled to the pleasure-pain of being inside her; his mind recoiled with the sudden unmistakable realization of her virginity.

"Good God, Elizabeth! I had no idea...."

"Hush." She silenced him with the press of her lips to his mouth. "It's all right. I wanted it to happen...with you. I still do. The pain is nothing."

"But..."

"No," she murmured against his lips. "That pain is gone. But I still hurt. Help me, Lyon." She slid her hands to his hips, urging him deeper into her. "Make the hurt go away. Take me away with it."

Lyon couldn't have refused if he'd wanted to...and refusing was the last thing he wanted to do. Given free rein, he went wild, wilder than he had ever before allowed himself in an encounter with any woman.

By the time it was over, their bodies were slick with perspiration, shimmering in the slanting silvery glow of moonlight.

It was the most shattering, satisfying, yet oddly self-generating experience Lyon had ever lived through. Before his breathing resumed at a normal rate, he felt an overwhelming need to live through it again.

Elizabeth felt him quicken inside her. Raising her head from his damp shoulder, she gazed at him from passion-shadowed eyes lit from within by a spark of confusion and amazement.

"Again?" Incredulity colored her soft voice.

"Yes." Lyon felt like a giant...a humble giant. "But I don't want to hurt you."

"Too late." A smile curved her kiss-pinkened lips. "I'm hurting now."

Lyon went still with remorse. He grabbed her waist to lift her away from him. "I'm sorry...I..."

"No." She shook her head and pressed down, resisting his effort to move her from him. "I'm hurting again, like before. In the same way you are." She lowered her head to him, glided the tip of her tongue along his lower lip. "Love me again, Lyon."

Lyon thrilled to the sweet sound of Elizabeth's voice, imploring him to love her, every night that remained of his vacation. Long before the two weeks had elapsed, he knew he was hopelessly, irrevocably in love for the first time in his life.

Elizabeth filled his days and nights, and his mind, with warmth and tenderness, laughter and loving. She was gentle and bright, quick and compassionate. She was everything he had ever secretly dreamed of, hoped for, longed for in a woman—his woman.

Lyon poured out his love for Elizabeth the night before he was to return to New York. Her response was immediate, satisfying, arousing.

"Oh, Lyon, I love you, too," she cried, throwing her arms around his neck and clinging, as if to keep him with her, close to her, forever. "I love you so much." Her mouth sought his, with a hunger bordering on desperate. "Take me with you...please."

"I can't, darling, you know that," he said, denying himself as well as her. He wanted her with him, needed her with him, but she was still so young, and he hadn't as yet spoken to her parents, his own parents. But, Lord, being parted from her, if only for a week or two, was going to be more than difficult, it would be hell.

"I'll try to get back next weekend," he promised, his own greedy mouth tasting her cheeks, her eyelids, her temples. "If I can, I'll call you to let you know what time to expect me." His hands roamed with a restless, compulsive need to imprint the feel of her on his skin.

"I'll be here, waiting," she vowed, clasping his hips to bring him deeper, and yet deeper into her. "Waiting just for you," she moaned, arching high into his hard-driving thrust. "Just for you."

"Elizabeth." Lyon's voice was hoarse from the strain he was exerting to control his release until she had attained her own.

"Oh, my love. Lyon!"

Elizabeth's muffled scream of ecstasy shattered his restraint. Clasping her shuddering body to him, Lyon soared with her into paradise.

"You okay, young man?"

The sharp concern of the male voice brought Lyon crashing back to the present. He blinked, shook his head to get his mental marbles into gear, and offered the stranger a weak smile.

"Yes, thank you." His forehead was wet with sweat unrelated to the eighty-plus air temperature.

The elderly gentleman hesitated with his hand on the Elegant Man's ornate doorknob. "You're awful pale. Heat get to you?"

Lyon gratefully grabbed at the excuse. "Guess so," he agreed, shrugging. "Spoiled by air-conditioning, I suppose, in the home, office and car."

"Mmm, heard that's how it happens." The man nodded sagely. "You're sure you're all right now?"

Lyon drew a deep, memory-dispersing breath. "Yes, sir, I'm fine. Thanks again for your concern."

The old man smiled, turned the knob, and pushed open the door to the shop. "We're all stumbling through this life together, son. A little show of concern now and again lightens the load."

Does it? Lyon reflected as he watched the man disappear into the cool interior of the shop. Did he feel any lighter for the kindly gentleman's concern?

Seeking the cause of his pale, sweaty condition, Lyon focused his intent stare on the young woman propped against the parking meter, now tapping her sandaled foot with obvious mounting impatience.

Did he feel any lighter?

Not hardly.

What Lyon felt was curiosity—tinged by unacknowledged jealousy. Who was Elizabeth waiting for with such apparent eager restlessness?

A man?

Another man?

She certainly hadn't waited for him ten years ago.

Lyon's lips flattened into a harsh, unrelenting line as, coolly, deliberately, he recalled the anxious weeks following his return to New York.

Having decided that two weeks were sufficient to restore his son to full working order, his father had a schedule ready for Lyon that would make a slave master blanch with envy.

In love, revitalized, buoyant with the sheer joy of life, Lyon accepted his father's challenge with a jaunty smile. Of course, since his marching orders included three European countries, he was also forced to accept the realization that he could not possibly make it back to the States, and Cantrell, by the weekend, or indeed several weekends to come.

Lyon called Elizabeth at once to explain.

Elizabeth, while assuring him she understood, assuaged his own sense of disappointment, and effectively stroked his ego by softly, fervently, confessing how very much she missed having him close to her, part of her life, in her arms, in her body.

Thus motivated, Lyon worked like an overzealous SWAT team, completing his six-week assignment in five weeks and one day. At every opportunity that presented itself, he rushed to a phone to call her. He'd actually spoken to her on one occasion...the first. After that, she was either not there or, mysteriously for the past week and a half, he'd received no answer at all. By the time he boarded the plane for New York, he was wracked by questions, doubts and a steadily mounting unnamed anxiety.

Where was Elizabeth? Was she all right? Had something happened? And why the hell didn't anyone ever answer the phone?

He dialed her number again the minute he arrived at his uptown apartment...again there was no answer.

Tasting real fear for the first time in his adult life, Lyon roared out of New York in his Cadillac less than half an hour later, breaking the speed limit as he made a mad dash for Cantrell.

Elizabeth was gone. But not only Elizabeth, the entire family was gone. The house stood abandoned, empty. So swiftly had the move occurred, the utilities had not yet been disconnected.

Worst of all, nobody—not one friend, neighbor, mere acquaintance or resident—appeared to know where the Wares had gone. Other than the useless information that Chuck Ware and his bride, Jennifer, were somewhere in the Middle East, not even Hunt could offer a clue as to where and why the Ware family had made such an abrupt departure.

Lyon was frantic with worry. He searched, questioned, and hired private investigators to do the same. All to no avail. There wasn't a trace.

Eventually, Lyon was left with little option but to face the truth. The Wares, and Elizabeth in particular, didn't want to be found.

His eyes glittering like the jewel they resembled, his grim mouth twisting into a grimace, Lyon stared at the only woman he had ever loved.

Elizabeth.

Thinking her name seared his mind and set a torch to his embittered soul.

She was more beautiful than he remembered.

She glanced at her watch, then looked up at the doorway to the barber shop. A brilliant smile lit her face... and sent a chill racing through Lyon.

Who was he? Who was this man she had waited for with such eagerness and impatience. What did he look like, this... this person with the power to bring such a radiant glow of love to Elizabeth's beautiful face?

The thought stabbing at him, Lyon shifted his gaze to the shop's doorway, and felt his breath lodge in his suddenly constricted throat.

A tall, lanky boy of nine or ten stepped from the shop and loped across the sidewalk to Elizabeth. A grin flashed as he turned to face her.

Lyon felt as if he had taken a hard right jab to his solar plexus.

Looking at the boy was like looking into a twenty-seven-year, time-warped mirror at his own boyhood image.

Lyon's senses swam. *It couldn't be,* he screamed in silent anguish.

Pain was a living entity inside his chest.

Could it be?

His thoughts fractured.

Ten years. Ten years.

Good God!

Could it be?

It had to be!

The evidence was right there in front of him.

His own face—staring him in the face.

That boy was his son!

Damn Elizabeth.

That bitch!

Two

"Are we almost there?"

Elizabeth spared a glance from the winding back road to the boy sprawled in an awkward-looking position within the safety belt in the bucket seat beside her. He looked tired, and not surprisingly so; it was now late afternoon and they had been on the road since midmorning. They had made only one rest stop during the drive from their home in the southeast corner of Pennsylvania to the northeast corner of the state.

"Almost." A soft smile relieved the lines of weariness bracketing her eyes and mouth. "Are you getting hungry?'' she asked, even though she knew the answer; her son was always hungry.

"Yeah." He grinned, evoking images of another male, images she refused to let linger in her mind. "I hope Aunt Jen has supper ready."

"She probably has...if I know your cousins," Elizabeth said, replacing the adult male image in her mind with those of her three young, boisterous and also always hungry nephews.

"Maybe she made spaghetti." His dark blue eyes gleamed with anticipation. "Or some lasagna." He smacked his lips. "Aunt Jen makes the best!"

"That's because her mother taught her," Elizabeth said, chiding herself for the twinge of envy she felt for her son's unqualified admiration for her sister-in-law's cooking skills.

"Huh?"

"Aunt Jen's mother is Italian," she explained. "She taught her how to cook."

"Oh." He pondered the information a moment, then said, artlessly, "Too bad she didn't teach you, too."

"Mitchell David Ware!" Elizabeth exclaimed with mock exasperation. "I'm a very good cook, and you know it. At least, you always gobble up any and every meal I put in front of you."

"Yeah." His grin flashed again, revealing hard, even white teeth, and recalling the unwelcome image of the one male visage she didn't want to remember.

Of course, forgetting that male visage was difficult—if not flat out impossible—since the near carbon copy of it lived in the animated features of her son.

"You make the best roast beef," he went on, rubbing his concave belly. "And chocolate cake. And barbecued chicken. And homemade waffles. And—"

"It's a good thing we've arrived," Elizabeth inserted in a teasing voice, turning onto the driveway leading to the mountain retreat her brother had purchased a few years ago. "Another couple of minutes, and you'd be chewing the seat in a feeding frenzy."

"Oh, decent!" Mitch cried his latest, and already overused expression to describe the wood and glass bilevel house he was seeing for the first time. Then, in a flurry of excited motion, he released the buckle on the safety belt, and the door handle, and went tumbling from the car, seemingly all legs, arms and enthusiasm. "Hurry up, Mom," he called impatiently.

Before Elizabeth could voice a chastising response, the air was rent by loud welcoming whoops as three young dynamos burst from the house.

"Hey, Mitch, where ya been?"

"We've been waitin' and waitin'."

"Yeah, what kept ya?"

The questions came rapid-fire and simultaneously from Elizabeth's three nephews, the eight-year-old twins and their six-year-old brother.

"I hadda get my hair cut in town," Mitch groused in explanation.

"What for?" Chuck, the eldest of the twins by a full five minutes, demanded, eyeing his cousin's closely cropped hair.

"Yeah, you look like a cue ball," Bobby, the younger twin, opined, grimacing.

"Yeah, like the ones with Dad's pool table at home." Billy, the "baby," threw in his two cents' worth.

"My mom made me," Mitch said in tones of injury and disgust.

"Nasty old mom, anyway." The wryly voiced assessment came from the pixie-faced woman exiting the house. "How'd you get so mean, anyhow?"

"Lots of practice." Laughing, Elizabeth stepped away from the car and into the open arms of her best friend and sister-in-law. "You look great, Jen. How do you keep from going gray with these three heathens around?"

"Lots of hair dye," Jen retorted, stepping back to run a quick, comprehensive glance over Elizabeth's ultraslim body and beautiful face. "And you're not exactly looking like dog meat, yourself. How in the world do you manage to forever remain a size seven?"

"Oh, nothing to it," Elizabeth said, flicking her hand dismissively. "I don't eat."

"You never did," Jen reminded her. "You always were the only friend I ever had who wasn't addicted to food, and ate to live, rather than vice versa."

"Food!" Mitch pounced on the only word of interest to him in the conversation.

"Yeah, food!" Chuck picked up the cry.

"Food, food," the other two chanted.

Elizabeth slanted a droll look at her sister-in-law. "Do you get the feeling these uncivilized characters are trying to tell us something?"

"Mmm." Jen returned the look. "I'd say it's a good thing I have dinner simmering on the stove."

"What's for dinner, Aunt Jen?" Mitch asked, his sapphire eyes sparkling with eager anticipation.

"Scetty and meatballs!" Billy informed in a gleeful shout. "With garlic bread and salad and red Jell-O with fruit mixed in for dessert."

"Way to go, Aunt Jen! What a friend!" Mitch yelled, dancing in circles while exchanging high-fives with each cousin in turn.

"Jen, Jen, she's our friend!" Chuck began to chant, circling around behind Mitch.

"Jen, Jen, she's our friend!" Bobby and Billy took up the jubilant cry, and the disjointed body movements of the other two boys.

The youngsters' performance was all that was required to chase away Elizabeth and Jen. Exchanging
dry looks and wryly amused smiles, they escaped into
the momentary quiet of the house.

"He's back, you know."

Dinner was long since over; the boys had finally
given up the battle against sleep. Jen's softly voiced
comment broke the blessed silence.

"Back?" Elizabeth frowned and looked away from
the magazine article she was skimming to glance out
the wide living-room window, expecting to see the
beam of a car's headlights slicing through the darkness. The night beyond the pane remained undisturbed by either light of the sound of an approaching
vehicle. Her frown deepened as she shifted her puz-
zled gaze to Jen, curled up in the plushly padded chair
opposite her. "Who's back?"

"The mountain lion." Jen's voice and expression
held wry acceptance. "I understand that's how the
locals now refer to him."

Alarm jangled through Elizabeth. A sense of fore-
boding sprang into her mind, and her thoughts flew to
Mitch, peacefully asleep on a foldaway cot in Billy's
room. An image of Mitch formed, clear and sharp, a
boyish replica of the man who had fathered her son,
and then abandoned her with an insulting payoff of a
check for a shocking sum—as if mere money, regard-

less how large an amount, could erase his involvement, his obligation, his responsibilities ... and her devotion, commitment, and her ultimate shame.

Elizabeth wasn't aware of slowly moving her head back and forth in a silent denial. Fate, or coincidence, couldn't be so cruel as to have her return to her hometown after a ten-year absence, only to find the man she had been avoiding all those years had returned, as well.

"The mountain lion?" Elizabeth repeated the phrase, hanging onto denial for all she was worth. She glanced again at the window. The darkness shrouded the near mountain, but she knew it was there, the private domain of the powerful Cantrell family, looming over the valley and the small town nestled within it. Her throat and lips went dry; she moistened them with a quick swallow and a nervous flick of her tongue. "There's a wild lion on the prowl on the mountain?"

"Prowling and growling ... if what I've heard since I arrived last week can be believed."

"What ... have you heard?" Elizabeth had to force the question past the painful tightness constricting her throat; but it was imperative that she ask, hear whatever Jen had picked up over the past week.

"That he's changed, withdrawn, more aloof than before, harsh and hard, not at all the same man."

There, it was said, out in the open. Not a wild animal, stalking the mountain, but a man, a powerful man, an animal without fangs or claws, but a lion, nonetheless.

"Lyon." Elizabeth's voice was barely audible.

"Yes." Jen dipped her head in acknowledgment. "Lyon Cantrell."

Sheer panic clawed at Elizabeth's nerves, and she had to grip the chair arms to keep from leaping up, to run as fast and as far as possible. Her heart raced beneath the muscles contracting in her chest. Her breath came in short, uneven spurts.

"I've got to go." Her eyes moved rapid-fire, darting glances around the quiet room, as if searching for a large shadow hidden within the depths of deeper shadows. "I've got to get Mitch and go."

"Beth." Jen's voice was low-pitched but sharp, barbed to snare Elizabeth's attention. "You look like you're ready to shatter. Pull it together," she ordered, not unkindly. "Mitch is asleep. You can't just roust him and go tearing off at this time of the night."

Elizabeth shifted her haunted gaze to her friend. "I must. I can't take the chance of running into him, and if I stay he might see me in town or somewhere...." Her voice faded, and her eyes grew wide with fear. "Jen, he might see Mitch! I can't let him see Mitch!"

"Calm down." Jen's voice was even sharper than before. "And stay put," she commanded when Elizabeth made an obvious move to spring from the chair. "So, okay, you're here, and he's here and, from all indications, he's here to stay, a permanent resident. And, since you'll be here for a month, chances are you very likely will run into him. So what? Lyon disclaimed any and all interest ten years ago." Jen's normally gentle voice took on a rough edge. "If you should run into him, you can look him straight in the eyes and tell him in no uncertain terms to buzz off."

Elizabeth was hovering on the very edge of the chair cushion, ready to bolt. Her fingers clenched and opened spasmodically on the chair arms. Her teeth punished her soft lower lip. Her eyes contained ten years' worth of fear of the possibility she now faced.

"Jen, you don't understand," she whispered in a cry of desperation. "You don't know—"

"I do know," Jen said, cutting her off in a commiserating tone before going on with sudden impatience. "Darn, I wish Chuck was here, instead of traipsing around Europe for his company. He's been itching for ten years to confront Lyon." She gave a slight understanding smile. "Don't know? Oh, Beth, Chuck and I know how bad it was for you. We were there, remember?"

Remember? Endorsing Jen's wish that her brother had been able to join them for this vacation, Elizabeth closed her eyes and concentrated on suppressing an incipient bubble of hysterical laughter. Remember? Dear God! If only she could forget.

"I've been saving a ridiculously expensive bottle of wine for a special occasion."

The creaking of Jen's chair as she pushed herself from it barely penetrated the misery gripping Elizabeth; Jen's voice hardly rippled the surface of her mind.

"I'm going to pop the cork on that bottle right now. We could both use a drink."

Elizabeth registered Jen's remark on one level of her consciousness. But her sister-in-law's voice went unheard deeper inside, where memory forever lived, retaining the power to decimate her emotional equilibrium.

Elizabeth's mental world tilted. Helpless against the magnetic pull, she slid into the murky depths of as yet unhealed and still painful retrospection.

Elizabeth was happy, as happy as only a young, healthy girl could be on a warm and cloudless summer day. Her high school days were over. It was her birthday, the long anticipated eighteenth.

A celebration was planned . . . ostensibly a farewell gathering for her brother Chuck, who had accepted a promotion and hefty hike in salary from his company—along with a transfer to one of the Arab Emerate states. Chuck was leaving, taking Jen with him, directly after their wedding, scheduled to take place in a few weeks.

But there was also planned a party within a party in celebration of Elizabeth's eighteenth birthday. She wasn't supposed to know about it. Keeping her knowledge and excitement contained had not been easy.

Appearing surprised when the birthday greetings rang out required the second best acting performance of Elizabeth's eighteen years on earth. But, by far, her most outstanding performance was given when Chuck's friend, Hunt Canon, arrived on the party scene with a guest in tow.

Lyon Cantrell.

Merely thinking his name induced a delicious shiver along Elizabeth's spine. Having him show up at her birthday party was nearly her undoing.

Elizabeth had been distantly aware of Lyon from the time she was in grade school, though he didn't attend the local schools or hang out with the other kids his age, and had made no close friendships with any of them. She fell in love with him the summer she was fifteen.

The original emotion she had felt was pure hero worship for the tall, muscularly lean, blue-eyed and tawny-haired young Adonis. To Elizabeth's innocent eyes, Lyon Cantrell was the picture of male perfection.

Even she had expected the emotion to dissipate with time and budding maturity. It hadn't. Quite the contrary, in fact. Although Elizabeth had only seen him at brief intervals during the ensuing three years, the emotion of hero worship had matured right along with her, deepening into the sweet painful love that only an adult woman can feel for a mature man.

Having Lyon there, close to her, hearing him wish her a happy birthday, was for Elizabeth infinitely sweeter than the mounds of flowered icing on her elaborately tiered birthday cake.

Lyon had presented to her a gift of a delicate, finely wrought gold chain bracelet. Extending her arm to him, she had asked him to fasten it around her wrist, and made a silent vow never to remove it.

Elizabeth had been thrilled when Lyon had asked to see her again, and without hesitation had agreed to a secret tryst with him. She had made eager, soul-satisfying love with him every night of the time remaining of his vacation, her only adornment the shimmering gold bracelet coiled around her slim wrist.

Five weeks later Elizabeth had broken her vow, and the bracelet's clasp, when she'd torn it from her wrist and flung it from her. Five minutes after that, on her knees and sobbing, she had crawled over every inch of her bedroom floor until she'd found it.

Calling herself all kinds of a gullible fool, Elizabeth had placed the chain in the velvet box and buried it at the very bottom of the storage carton containing all the items of memorabilia with which she couldn't bear to part. The velvet case had remained there since that terrible day.

That terrible day.

A shudder quaked through Elizabeth's trembling body. Even after ten years, the memory of that fateful day retained the power to slash her emotions into ribbons of searing pain and humiliation.

She had given herself, body and soul, to Lyon in love and joy. Lyon had taken her gift and twisted it into ugly bitterness and shame.

How could she have been so deceived?

The question had tormented Elizabeth throughout every day of those intervening ten years, first as a conscious demand, then later as an unconscious, unformed, but ever-present question mark.

She had truly believed that Lyon loved her as much as she loved him. And feeling secure within her belief, Elizabeth had gloried in their uninhibited physical expression of that shared love.

But Lyon had not loved her, or even cared for her. Nor had he possessed the common decency to reject her, and their unborn child, in person. On that fateful, terrible day, Lyon had sent his father, checkbook in hand, as his emissary.

Thunder rumbled in the distance—and reverberated inside Elizabeth's pounding head. The onslaught of memory blows had given her an excruciating mind-ache.

"Beth . . . are you all right?"

Elizabeth shook off the chains of reverie, blinked, and focused her shadowed eyes on Jen. "No," she admitted, wincing as another rumble of thunder stalked around the mountain. "I'm scared."

"Of Lyon? Or the storm?" Jen arched her brows and, stepping forward, held out a fluted glass filled to the rim with pale gold wine.

"Of Lyon." Saying his name hurt and caused a tremor in the hand she extended to take the glass.

"Why?" Jen's frown was fierce. "As the old saying goes . . . what can he do to you?"

A sliver of ice trickled down Elizabeth's spine. The memory of what Lyon could do, had done, was as strong as if it had happened yesterday and not ten years ago. In that instant she could feel the clamorous sensations only Lyon had the power to arouse inside her . . . sensations both terrifying and exciting.

"Mitch," Elizabeth whispered, unwilling to admit, even to Jen, the sensual hold Lyon still possessed over her. "I don't want him to see Mitch . . . ever."

Shaking her head, Jen sighed and sank into her chair, setting the wine swirling precariously in her glass. "So you'll run away. Again."

"I must."

"For how long?" Jen took a long, bracing swallow of wine. "You're not a fugitive, a criminal, for heaven's sake! Why should you continue to disrupt your life avoiding him?" Her voice had grown harsh, hard with conviction. "*He* was the one at fault, not you."

Elizabeth wet her parched lips with a sip from her glass. "I know, but..." Her voice faded and she shivered as yet another low growl of thunder crawled over the mountain. The storm was moving nearer; she could feel the pressure from the roiling atmosphere—at least, that's what she told herself the feeling of expanding pressure inside her was from.

The lion on the mountain was a summer storm, nothing more, Elizabeth assured herself, repressing another shiver. A storm that would quickly pass.

"Oh, this makes me so damn mad!"

Jen's sudden outburst snagged Elizabeth's attention. She blinked in confusion, shot a quick glance at the window, then frowned. "The storm?"

"Yes." Jen sat forward, her expression and voice intense. "But not the one out there—" she flicked a hand at the window "—the one seething inside you. Dammit, it isn't fair." She raked a hand through her short curly hair. "I know how much you were looking forward to this vacation, this time to be with Mitch. You've worked so very hard these past ten years, finishing your schooling, raising Mitch. And you've achieved so much, earning your wings, securing a position with Mid-Continental, and then making second officer in a little over a year." Frustration underscored Jen's tense voice. "And it just isn't fair or right that you should now feel an urgency to run and hide...and all because of him." Her lip curled over her last word.

Elizabeth had to concede that her sister-in-law's point was valid. She had worked hard, damned hard, even if she had loved every minute of the work of raising her son while attending the flight school, and then the rigorous classes given to prospective pilot employees by Mid-Continental Airlines.

And she had achieved a great deal, Elizabeth acknowledged without a shred of conceit. Making second officer after little more than a year with the company was an accepted, creditable accomplishment. Of course, it hadn't hurt that she not only adored her son but loved to fly. But even so, she had worked damn hard, and had not only looked forward to, but needed this vacation.

Why had Lyon returned, now, after all these years, to the scene of his crime...so to speak?

"I wonder why Lyon decided to come back here," Elizabeth mused aloud. "It seems odd that he's come back now, when he never spent much time here before."

"Well, I suppose it's partly because of his father's death."

Elizabeth sent Jen a surprised look. "Mr. Cantrell passed away?"

"Mmm." Jen nodded. "About six months ago, so I was told. Massive heart attack." Her usually tender mouth twisted. "Couldn't have happened to a more deserving man."

Elizabeth felt she should protest Jen's harsh condemnation, but in truth, she honestly could not. She felt nothing but bitterness for the autocratic, overbearing old man—alive or dead.

"You said partly because of his father's death," Elizabeth recalled. "Have you heard other reasons for Lyon deciding to remain here?"

"Plenty." Jen laughed. "You know how it's always been around here. Everybody knows everybody else's business. And rumor is rife about Lyon."

Elizabeth hardly noticed the closer, louder bang of thunder. She was too intent on prying information out of her sister-in-law. "So, give. What have you heard? What's the general consensus?"

Jen's smile was wry. "There isn't one general consensus. There's a whole bunch of speculation." She gave an airy wave of her hand. "But there seems to be one common absolute about Lyon." She paused to savor a deep swallow of wine, then refill her glass.

Elizabeth sighed. "Are you going to tell me, or must I guess?"

"Do you want to hear every descriptive adjective I've heard in reference to him?"

"Might as well," Elizabeth said, steeling herself for the worst.

Jen shrugged. "Okay, here goes. What I've heard is that Lyon has become...cold, hard, ruthless, heartless, withdrawn, severe, austere, demanding, arrogant and, overall, tough to the very outside edge of enough." Her voice turned droll. "Kinda sounds like the hero—or antihero—of a typical low-budget spaghetti Western, doesn't it?"

"Yes." Elizabeth exhaled in an effort to ease the increased tightness in her throat and chest. "He also sounds a little scary."

Jen made a rude, snorting noise. "Depends on what scares you. Personally, I think he sounds like a jerk."

But then, you aren't the mother of his illegitimate son, either.

Keeping the retort to herself, Elizabeth prompted, "You said there was plenty of speculation as to the reasons for the changes in his personality."

"Lots of speculation." Jen laughed. "Small towns are a wonder. Practically every person I've talked to has a different theory. Amazing. One believes it's due to the sudden death of his father. Another thinks it's because of the stress and strain from all the years he ate, slept and lived for his work and the company. The closest thing to a general consensus I heard was the belief that the drastic change in Lyon is primarily due to the defection of his wife and subsequent failure of his marriage, and following so soon as it had on the death of his mother."

Shock tore a quaking path through Elizabeth's body. She didn't know why that fact struck such a forceful emotional blow, but it did. She did know she didn't want to examine the possible causes for her intense reaction to the information. "Lyon's divorced?"

"Uh-huh." Jen nodded. "About three, four years now. The marriage only lasted a year or so, they tell me."

"Three or four years," Elizabeth repeated, frowning in confusion. "But I thought... believed... Dad, Mother, we were led to believe..."

"What?" Jen asked when Elizabeth's voice faded.

Elizabeth's face grew warm with remembered humiliation. "Mr. Cantrell came to the house ten years ago, after Dad talked to him on the phone when he got impatient with not being able to contact Lyon. Dad was so angry, he told Mr. Cantrell over the phone that I was—" She paused to swallow against the brakish taste of shame clogging her throat.

"Go on," Jen urged, leaning forward in her chair.

It was incredible how much it still hurt, after all these years. Elizabeth drew a shuddering breath. "He told Mr. Cantrell that I was pregnant and that Lyon

was the father.'' Her soft lips flattened into a hard line.
''Mr. Cantrell said he would relay the information to
Lyon. Two days later, Mr. Cantrell showed up at the
house—'' her lip curled ''—ready to cut a deal.''

''The payoff.''

''Yes.'' Elizabeth sighed. ''He was very nice, very
polite, very sympathetic.'' She closed her eyes, fighting an overwhelming surge of painful memories, and
the sting of bitter tears.

''Are you calling my daughter a liar?'' Elizabeth's
father, Ralph, demanded. His thin body was taut with
anger; his normally sallow complexion glowed bright
with outraged color.

''No, no,'' Mr. Cantrell said in soothing tones, his
handsome, patrician face drawn in lines of regret.
''But, as a father, also, I am certain you can understand my hesitation to accuse my son of lying. The
announcement is imminent of his engagement and
forthcoming marriage to Miss Leslie Broadworth,
whose family has been close to ours for many years.''
He lifted his shoulders in a gesture of helplessness.
''What can I do?''

Ralph appeared on the point of exploding. ''But
dammit, man, your son is responsible here! Lyon is an
adult. Elizabeth is little more than a child. It should be
obvious to you, sir, that your son took advantage of
an innocent girl.''

Mr. Cantrell's expression altered, hardened, quivering with indignation. "My son, sir, was raised to be an honorable gentleman!"

"He's the father!" Ralph shouted.

"He denies involvement!" Mr. Cantrell retorted.

Ralph's entire body shook from the effects of his searing fury. "We can get a court order for a blood test to prove—"

"No!" Elizabeth had heard enough. Lyon did not want her, or the child they had created together. He was going to marry another woman—a more acceptable woman, whose family was long connected to the Cantrells. The knowledge of his perfidy was devastating to her emotions and pride. She could not, would not, humiliate herself further by forcing him to comply with legal action.

"What do you mean, *no?*" Her father turned on her. "Don't you understand? He's deserting you. Letting you face the future alone with his bastard. The son of a—"

"Ralph," Elizabeth's mother, Gloria, cut him off in a soft voice heavy with defeat. "Name calling will prove nothing." She turned to stare at the older man, her eyes shadowed by disappointment and concern. "I...liked and trusted your son, Mr. Cantrell, but—"

"Thank you, Mrs. Ware. I—" he began.

"But," Gloria continued as if she hadn't heard. "I see now that my trust was misplaced. If it were up to me, I, too, would insist on a paternity test." She sighed and turned to look at Elizabeth. "But it's not up to me. It is for my daughter to decide."

Elizabeth felt abandoned, shattered, shocked beyond the mere outburst of tears. Lyon did not love her, had never loved her. He was marrying another—socially acceptable—woman. Elizabeth wanted to run, hide, throw up. All that was left to her were the tattered remnants of her scored pride. Lifting her chin, she bravely met the three pairs of eyes trained on her.

"I will not agree to a court order," she said in a small but adamant voice.

Then her father did explode. "Elizabeth ... goddammit, girl, will you think! Do you realize what you'll be letting yourself in for? You'll be tossing away all your plans for the future, for college, flying—"

"Under the circumstances," Mr. Cantrell interrupted. "I am willing to offer my assistance."

The subsequent monetary offer he mentioned stunned Ralph and Gloria, and deepened the sickness pervading Elizabeth's being. The sum was shockingly exorbitant, and to Elizabeth, a silent admission of Lyon's guilt.

Fighting the nausea clawing at her throat, Elizabeth shook her head and choked out one word. "No."

But in this refusal she was overruled. Even her mother stood firm against her.

A deal was struck. The Ware family was bought and paid for, right down to agreeing to pulling up stakes, folding their domestic tent and slipping quietly and unobtrusively out of town.

"I always wondered exactly what happened at that meeting."

Unaware that she had been reliving the memory aloud, Elizabeth stared at Jen with surprise-widened eyes. "It was pretty awful," Elizabeth murmured.

"I can imagine," Jen said. "But, if nothing else, Cantrell's guilt money did enable you to support Mitch while you finished your education and training."

"Yes." Elizabeth smiled with faint cynicism. "So I can thank Lyon for my career as well as my son." Her beautiful face took on a glow of unadulterated love. "And I thank God every day of my life for the gift of Mitch, the blessing his father rejected."

"So why do you now feel you must run again?"

Elizabeth frowned her incomprehension. "What do you mean?"

"Lyon didn't want his son, right?"

"Yes." It still hurt Elizabeth to admit to that soul-destroying truth.

"Well, then..." Jen's smile was downright nasty. "If he should happen to run into you or Mitch while you're here, and he can't face the proof of his actions, or himself, this time let him be the one to run."

Once again pride came to bolster Elizabeth's flagging spirit. "Yes," she said in a tone of enlightenment. "Why should I run, give up my vacation? You're absolutely right. If Lyon doesn't like what he might see, that's his problem. Let him run away from it."

Jen gave a victorious whoop. "You'll stay?"

Elizabeth lifted her chin, and her glass.

"Yes, come hell, high water...or Cantrell, the mountain lion, I'll stay."

Three

––––––

Lyon stalked through the spacious rooms of the huge English manor style house like the predator he had been compared to by the local residents.

He had slept little and eaten less during the twenty-odd hours that had elapsed since he had been stunned by the sight of that boy with Elizabeth.

Seeing Elizabeth, more beautiful than before, had been shocking enough. Then to have that initial shock compounded by the sight of the boy....

Lyon cursed beneath his breath—in a soft tone that had more the sound of a feral snarl.

The boy was his, of his flesh, of his blood, of his loins. Lyon knew it with a gut-wrenching certainty.

The timing was right, for the boy looked to be about nine, Lyon raged in silent agony. Why hadn't he known about the child? Why had she disappeared without a trace, without telling him she was pregnant?

Damn Elizabeth!

A wildness sizzled through Lyon, denying him rest or surcease from infuriating speculation. His thoughts pelting his mind like sharp stones, he prowled along the wide second-story corridors and down the broad, curving staircase to the parqueted foyer. Spitting mad, he stormed from one elegantly appointed room to another, seeing nothing, feeling nothing but the fury consuming him, cursing and condemning the woman he had never stopped wanting.

I'll throttle her.

The thought brought a grim smile of satisfaction to Lyon's lips. His fingers itched to close around her delicate white throat. He flexed his fingers and strode through the long, multipaned doors leading onto the side patio and the English rose gardens beyond.

"No." Unaware of speaking aloud, or the heady scent of roses in first bloom, Lyon came to an abrupt halt on the graveled pathway.

Throttling was too quick, too easy, too lenient a punishment for the magnitude of Elizabeth's cruel deceit and betrayal.

Cold-hearted bitch.

His raving senses inflamed, immune to the peace and tranquillity of his surroundings, Lyon strode the crisscrossing paths, cataloging the sins of commission and omission perpetrated against him by the woman he had honored above all others.

Elizabeth had vowed undying love for him.

Lyon's lip curled.

She had promised to wait—forever if need be—for him to complete the mission assigned to him by his father.

His lip curled higher, baring his hard white teeth.

Elizabeth had denied him the right to his only child for nine long years.

A low growl vibrated from his throat.

He had given her his absolute trust, and she had betrayed it. Even worse, he had given her his unconditional love, and Elizabeth had not only thrown his love back in his face, she had run away, very likely to practice her bewitching wiles on some—or many—other besotted trusting fools. But the most unforgivable of all her deceptions was the soul-tearing realization that she had taken his son with her.

She would pay, dearly, for her treachery.

The decision made, Lyon came to a stop, an old tenet whispering in his mind.

Let the punishment fit the crime.

Lyon's clamoring senses grew calm as he narrowed his eyes in concentration. He no longer felt the wisp of the warm, dry breeze, or the stinging hot rays from the high summer sun. A chill enveloped him, cool tendrils winding around the flame of anger, frosty fingers stroking the fury of passion into frigid rage. The cold penetrated to the depths of his being, encasing his heart, soul and mind in shimmering ice.

How best to exact justice?

Lyon's brow beetled in thought as he began strolling back to the house. What method of retribution could he employ to derive satisfaction? Whatever means he eventually chose would have to be severe, but not physical, like his initial impulse to throttle her. Oh, no. A psychological thrashing would be a sweeter form of reparation.

Several ideas immediately sprang to Lyon's mind. He summarily rejected them as either too involved or too convoluted.

He wanted something simple, but devastating.

But what?

Lyon's frown deepened, then suddenly cleared when the answer to his mental block struck him.

He didn't possess enough information. Ten years was a long time. Lyon hadn't a ghost of an idea as to how Elizabeth had spent those years.

"Idiot!" Chastising himself for allowing his emotions to cloud his intellect, Lyon picked up his pace and strode into the house, directly to the phone on the desk in the somber, book-lined library.

Any businessman worth his salt knew the folly of taking on a competitor without first availing himself of all the data he could garner.

Lifting the telephone receiver, he punched in the number of the same investigative firm he had often employed over the ten years since their unsuccessful attempt at finding the Ware family.

Lyon had never blamed the firm for the failure; the Wares had disappeared without a trace. This time the situation was different. Lyon knew where Elizabeth was; at any rate, he assumed she would be staying at the isolated house belonging to her brother Chuck. But, in addition to knowing her approximate whereabouts, Lyon had recalled something from his sight of her yesterday. It could amount to nothing, or it could be a valuable clue.

A cold, grim smile tilting his hard mouth, Lyon drew forth a mental picture of the shirt Elizabeth had been wearing, and the logo emblazoned on the chest.

Mid-Continental Airlines.

It might prove nothing more than a young woman's fashion whim. On the other hand, the logo just might prove to be the key the investigative firm needed to unlock the mystery of Elizabeth's activities for the past ten years.

Lyon brought the gleaming silver sports car to a purring stop off the side of the road beside a mailbox bearing the name Ware situated a few feet from the driveway leading to the glass and wood house.

The breeze carried the exuberant sound of young voices from the far side of the house. Lyon shifted his narrowed gaze to the corner of the house as the high-pitched voices drew nearer. A moment later four boys careered around the house in hot pursuit of a fast-rolling soccer ball.

Lyon's heart lurched at the sight of the lanky boy in the lead of the noisy group...the same boy he had seen lope to Elizabeth in town three long weeks ago.

The black and white ball was on a direct path toward the silver sports car. His throat dry, tight with emotion, excitement leaping along his nervous system, Lyon pushed open the door next to him and stepped from the car. Extending his foot, he blocked the ball's passage, preventing it from rolling under the car and down the sloping road.

"Hey, mister, thanks!" the lanky, tawny-haired youngster called, screeching to a halt in front of him.

"You're welcome," Lyon said in an emotion-husky tone, staring into the boy's face with hungry intensity. "It looks like you guys have a hot contest going here."

The boy grinned.

Lyon was lost, ensnared by paternal love.

* * *

"Lunch is ready." Elizabeth looked up from the pile of sandwiches she had just finished building. A frown of consternation drew her dark brows together. "Now where did those heathens disappear to?"

Jen paused in the act of stirring chocolate syrup into a large pitcher of milk to slant a grin at her. "The brave warriors of the never-quit tribe went chasing into the front yard after an escaping soccer ball." Her grin widened as her gaze settled on the mound of sandwiches. "Are we feeding four boys or the 42nd Airborne?"

Elizabeth laughed. "I was just wondering if I had made enough." She turned to the archway leading from the kitchen into the dining room and on into the front of the house. "While you finish swirling the milk, I'll go scream at them to come in and clean up for lunch."

"I'll toss the paper plates on the table," Jen called after her.

Elizabeth laughed. She was feeling good, relaxed and at ease after three weeks of not a sight or sound from Lyon Cantrell, plus Jen's brand of bracing company.

A frown knit her delicately arched brows as she neared the front door. It was awfully quiet out there. Had the boys galloped around to the backyard again?

She should have glanced out the window; it would have saved her from an instant of heart-stopping shock.

Elizabeth swung open the door and felt an uncanny sensation of her blood freezing into a solid mass inside her veins.

Lyon Cantrell was standing beside an expensive-looking silver sports car, laughing down into the bright-eyed face of her son . . . his son!

Dear God, no!

A protest was born in her mind and expelled from her constricted throat.

"Mitch!" Elizabeth's voice was shrill, sharp-edged with panic. "Come here at once."

"Huh?" Mitch swung around, his expression a picture of incomprehension. "This man was just ask-in—"

"You know you are not to speak to strangers," Elizabeth said, cutting him off. "Lunch is ready," she went on, sweeping a glance over the other three boys as she started along the flagstone walk toward them . . . and Lyon.

"Gee, Mom," Mitch groused, shifting his confused gaze between her and the stranger. "He only asked—"

This time it was Lyon who interrupted Mitch, speaking in a voice too low for Elizabeth to make out what he was saying to the boy.

"Okay," Mitch replied, shrugging his thin shoulders as if to say "Who could understand adults?" and loping after his cousins, already halfway to the house.

Elizabeth reached out a hand to touch his sheared tawny hair as he passed her, then continued along the walk, her blazing gaze fixed on the tall man waiting for her.

"Hello, Elizabeth."

"Stay away from him," Elizabeth ordered, ignoring his softly voiced greeting.

"I don't think so."

A chill feathered Elizabeth's skin, defeating the power of the noonday sunrays. Lyon had not raised his voice, nor altered his even tone, yet she sensed—felt—the strength of intent behind his mild response.

"I don't want you anywhere near my son," she fairly spat the words at him.

"Your son?" Lyon cocked one golden eyebrow. "Did it all by yourself, did you?"

"Yes," she hissed, trembling with remembered pain and fear of the extended labor she had borne... without the comforting support of her child's father. "I did it all by myself." Hanging onto her composure with every shred of control she possessed, she swept his too attractive form with a dismissive glance, then turned away. "I meant what I said. Stay away from him."

"No."

The steel inside Lyon's soft tone brought her to an abrupt halt in midstep. Fighting an inner command to run, hide, Elizabeth drew a ragged breath and turned back to confront him.

He smiled.

The chill feathering the surface of her skin seeped into the marrow of her bones.

"I want him."

"No." She could manage little more than a whispering croak. "No."

Lyon's smile faded into a grim, unrelenting, thin-lipped line. "He's my son," he said in a low fear-inducing voice. "And I want him."

"And I said no." Elizabeth drew herself upright, spine rigid, chin tilted in challenge, in a show of defiance that was sheer bravado. She prayed he wouldn't see through the facade to the panic building inside her. "He is mine. Mine. You cannot have him, or even see him, talk to him. I absolutely forbid it."

"Forbid it?" Lyon echoed, his mouth again curving into a parody of a smile. "Exactly how do you think you can enforce this dictum?"

"You have no legal rights," Elizabeth said in tones of desperation. "No proof of paternity. I'll get a court order of restraint," she threatened, grasping at straws.

His smile reflected predatory satisfaction. "A court order?" he purred, shaking his head. "I'm afraid you're too late. I have already set the legal wheels in motion."

"What do you mean?" Elizabeth had to push the words past the tightness closing her throat. "What legal wheels? What have you done?"

"I have submitted to the necessary blood tests," he replied with cruel bluntness. "And I have also instructed my attorney to petition the court for custody—sole custody—of my son."

"Sole..." Elizabeth's voice deserted her. Unaware of her actions, she moved her head from side to side and slowly began backing away from him.

"Forget it, Elizabeth." Though still low, his voice held the power of a flicking whip.

Elizabeth flinched. "Forget... what?"

"Running." He sneered. "It won't work this time. I know everything about you. Where you live. The company you work for. Everything, down to the exact number of times you've been with that recently divorced pilot you've been seeing for the past six weeks."

Jesse. Elizabeth had a flashing image of the carefree man she had been dating. She had not been *with* him...not in the manner Lyon's tone implied. She and Jesse had been to see a few movies, talked and laughed together over several impromptu dinners. That was all.

Jesse had a reputation with the ladies, in or out of the marital state. Elizabeth knew better than to take the man seriously. He was an easy-going companion, fun to be with, share surface conversations. The perfect escort for her, since Elizabeth wasn't interested in becoming involved in a deeper, more intimate relationship, not with Jesse, or any other man. She had learned her lesson well about the perfidy of the male of the species.

Staring into the unrelenting expression of her original teacher, Elizabeth fought a silent battle against the panic-induced nausea welling in her throat. At that moment she couldn't have responded to him if her very existence had depended upon it.

"Nothing to say?" Lyon taunted in a soft but grating tone that abraded Elizabeth's nerves. "No defense to make of the dashing, if promiscuous, flyboy?"

Already rattled by his sarcasm and superior attitude, Elizabeth went stiff with anger, and retaliated without prudence. "Jesse doesn't need me to defend him, or his sexual life-style."

Lyon's mouth curved into that damnable, chilling smile. "How interesting," he purred. "When we get to a custody hearing, I feel sure the judge will find that information interesting, as well."

"Jesse's sleeping arrangements have nothing whatever to do with me, or any supposed custody hearing," she blurted out in protest.

"No? I beg to differ." Lyon's voice dripped disdain. "I have exact dates, and the exact amount of time your Jesse spent in your apartment, late at night, while my son slept innocently in his bed."

Elizabeth experienced the terrifying sensation of the world closing in on her. Panic tore at her chest, as if trying to claw its way out.

There was nothing, nothing to those late-night visits. Coffee. A nightcap. Conversation. Nothing else, she wanted to scream at him. But the denial lodged in her tight throat, drowned in the pool of bile stinging the tender flesh lining her mouth.

Robbed of words, Elizabeth again shook her head back and forth in mute denial, not only of Lyon's accusations, but of the bizarre situation. Her thoughts were wild, frantic, disjointed.

This couldn't be happening. Why? Why, after all these years had Lyon decided to torment her? It wasn't right. It wasn't fair. Was there no justice?

In that instant her throat loosened enough to expel a portion of her inner turmoil.

"Why are you doing this?" Elizabeth demanded in a painful whisper. "Why are you harassing me?"

"Because I want my son." Lyon's voice was low, rough-edged, ragged with emotion. "And I intend to have him." He gave a soft burst of laughter that set the short hairs at her nape quivering. "You think this little chat is a form of harassment? You're in for a

shock, Elizabeth. I haven't yet begun to harass you."
He sent a cold-eyed gaze over her body that made her
skin shrivel and crawl. "But I will. Bank on it."

"Lyon, you can't do this." Elizabeth cringed inwardly at the pleading note in her voice. But she believed him, every word of his threat.

He chuckled; a nasty sound. "I can and I—"

"Beth?" Jen's call cut across Lyon's low voice.
"Are you all right?"

Elizabeth was hard pressed not to laugh, hysterically, uncontrollably. All right? She was anything but
all right. She was scared out of her wits.

"I—I..." she stammered, turning a helpless look
at the stern-faced woman hurrying along the path to
her. "Yes, I'm fine," Elizabeth lied in an attempt to
halt Jen's approach, and a confrontation between her
friend and Lyon.

Elizabeth's attempt fell short of the mark, far short
of the mark. Jen strode on, the expression on her face
a warning of the verbal battle to come.

"What do you want here?" she demanded of Lyon
as she came to a stop mere inches from him.

Clearly unimpressed by the other woman's fierce
scowl and hard tone of voice, Lyon gave her a dry look
of unconcern. "What's mine," he answered with
brutal bluntness. "I want my son."

Jen made a hissing sound as she drew in her breath.
"Indeed?" She raised one eyebrow in a haughty arch;

a trick Elizabeth had always envied and had never
been able to pull off. "Lots of luck."

"Yes, indeed." Lyon's smile proved he was neither
intimidated nor daunted by Jen's ridicule. "And luck
will have nothing to do with it."

Jen's eyes flared with the light of anger. "You're on
shaky ground here, Mr. Cantrell. You may own that
mountain, and most of the town and surrounding
area, but this is private property."

"Jen..." Elizabeth began, trying to head off her
friend, diffuse the tension crackling on the air.

Jen ignored her. Armed by the right of ownership,
friendship and sense of family, she was obviously
ready for war. "You are trespassing, Cantrell." The
deliberate omission of the term of respectful address,
as well as her scathing tones, were calculated to in-
sult. "I suggest that you get in your pretty little car,
and haul your...uh, self, off my property."

"This attitude isn't helping Elizabeth, you know,"
Lyon advised Jen.

"Jen, please," Elizabeth again made an effort to
diffuse her friend's anger. "I can handle—"

"No." Jen's slim hand sliced through the air. "I'm
doing what Chuck would do, if he were here." She
leveled a hard-eyed stare on Lyon. "Are you going to
remove yourself, or must I call on the state police to do
it for you?" She glanced at her watch. "You have exactly ten seconds to make up your mind."

"Whatever you say." Lyon did not appear to be intimidated or insulted. Quite the opposite, he seemed to be mildly amused. "You are the property owner." He shrugged, turned toward the car, pulled the door open, then, whipping around, pinned Elizabeth with a narrowed look. "I will expect you at the house this evening at eight. Be there."

"Now, wait a minute!" Jen protested.

"At...at your house?" Elizabeth asked in shocked disbelief.

Lyon inclined his head, and slid his long body behind the wheel. "At my house. At eight."

"No!" Jen said sharply.

"But... why?" Elizabeth cried out over the thunking sound of the slamming car door.

"Because I said so," Lyon replied through the open car window. He ran another dismissive overall look the length of her rigid body as he fired the engine. "Unless you want to run the risk of losing even the occasional visiting rights to Mitch, you'll be there." With that parting shot, he gunned the engine and tore away, leaving the two women choking on his dust.

"Now what in hell was that visiting rights babble all about?" Jen asked, sputtering and waving her hand in front of her face to clear the tan-clouded air.

Elizabeth swallowed, against the acrid taste of fear, as well as the arid dust. "He said he has instructed his law firm to file a claim for custody of Mitch."

"What!" Jen exclaimed. "He can't. Why, he doesn't have a legal leg to stand on." Concern darkened her eyes as she stared into Elizabeth's pale face. "Does he?"

"I . . . don't know." Elizabeth bit down hard on her lip. "Jen, he must have had an investigative profile done on me. He claims he knows everything about me, my life." She was forced to swallow once more. "I—I . . ."

"You're not thinking of going to his house?" Jen asked, correctly reading Elizabeth's uncertain expression. "Beth, you can't."

"I must!" Elizabeth wailed.

"Chuck would—*will*—have a fit."

"I know, but what else can I do?"

"Call your lawyer."

"I don't have a lawyer."

"Then call Chuck's lawyer!" Jen exploded. "I feel sure he's bluffing, Beth."

"Maybe." Elizabeth wet her lips. "But what if he isn't? I have to know."

Jen shook her head and stared down the now deserted and quiet road. "I wouldn't trust him any farther than I could throw him. That man is positively lethal."

Hearing her own opinion confirmed certainly didn't ease Elizabeth's feeling of trepidation. "I know."

Jen spun to give her a belligerent look. "You'd be crazy to walk into that particular Lyon's den."

"I know. I know," Elizabeth cried, beginning to feel badgered.

"Then don't go," Jen insisted.

"I must." Elizabeth's voice betrayed her growing desperation. "Jen, please try to understand. I have to know what Lyon is planning to do. Don't you see? Until I have some idea of exactly what I'm up against, I can't even begin to fight him."

"I suppose." Jen heaved a sigh of defeat, and yet she persisted. "But I still think you'll be making a mistake by going there."

"So do I," Elizabeth admitted, turning to walk back to the house. "But I don't see that I have much of a choice. I must do it for Mitch."

Jen gave up the argument—for then. But, at regular intervals throughout the afternoon and into early evening, whenever the four boys were out of earshot, she reiterated her objections to Elizabeth's decision to meet alone with Lyon Cantrell.

Although she was riddled with doubts herself, Elizabeth remained steadfast in her determination. She dreaded the very thought of facing Lyon on his own territory but, even more, she dreaded the alternative.

"Well, if you are set on doing this, at least let me go with you," Jen pleaded as a last resort when Elizabeth excused herself to get ready.

Elizabeth paused at the base of the short staircase to offer her friend a faint, appreciative smile. "And leave the boys alone in the house?"

Jen raked her fingers through her hair. "I can call a neighbor...someone," she said in a tone of voice rife with strain. "Beth, I don't trust him. The look of him." She visibly shuddered. "To be honest, Lyon Cantrell frightens the hell out of me."

"He frightens me, too," Elizabeth admitted. "But," she went on, squaring her drooping shoulders, "I'll drop dead before I ever let him know that."

What Elizabeth didn't admit, not even to herself, was the double threat Lyon posed to her. At a conscious level, Elizabeth was terrified of his confident-sounding threat of gaining sole custody of Mitch.

In addition, unacknowledged and hidden deep within her subconscious, lurked an awareness of him, a terrifying, sensual awareness of Lyon—the man.

Four

She had to be out of her mind.

Elizabeth sat still and anxious in the car, listening to the summer night noises and her own recurring, cautioning thought, contemplating the ramifications of the lousy timing of fate...her fate.

One week remained of her accrued month-long vacation. One seven-day week.

Elizabeth sighed. She had almost made it through the month. Almost. But then, almost didn't count...did it? And, because it didn't count, here she sat, her stomach busily tying itself in knots, dreading the coming confrontation, and fighting an impulse to turn the car around, race back to her brother's house, pack her bags, grab her son and run as if her very life depended on it.

Was she out of her stunned mind for obeying Lyon's imperial dictate?

The consideration had nagged at Elizabeth all along the twisting road that wound its way up the side of Cantrell's mountain.

As mountains went, this one was neither awesome nor very impressive. It didn't boast sheer cliff walls or snow-cropped, jagged peaks. It was tree-covered and rounded on top, quite like a humpback on the earth.

The Cantrell stronghold was nestled within the trees on the side of the mountain near the top, at the end of the curving road. Unlike the mountain itself, the huge structure was both awesome and impressive.

The great pile of gray stone that made up Lyon's house loomed over her, intimidating by its imposing appearance, its daunting size and its classic design. It looked like a castle of old.

Elizabeth fancied that at any moment she would hear the clatter of destrier hooves on the macadam driveway, followed by the appearance of a knight decked out in full battle array.

If it were the knight of the house, she mused, he would naturally be a black knight.

Sir Lyon Cantrell—the destroyer.

A shiver drew goose bumps to the surface of Elizabeth's skin, the sudden chill conflicting with the al-

ready present sheen of perspiration drawn from her
heated body by apprehension more than the steamy
effects of the sultry summer night.

Thunder rumbled in the distance, giving a low
warning of the approach of yet another storm, in an
unusual, seemingly storm-tossed summer.

Sir Lyon prowling the mountain?

Chiding herself for her overactive imagination,
girding herself for what might lay ahead, she gathered her courage and stepped out of the car.

Her watch read two minutes to eight, and Elizabeth was determined to present herself at Lyon's front
door at precisely eight o'clock.

Of course, there was no conventional doorbell—
that would be much too prosaic and common for the
wealthy and distinguished Cantrell family.

A large and heavy brass knocker in the shape of a
stag's head was centered on the thick oak door.

How predictable, Elizabeth thought wryly, attempting to bolster her flagging spirits. When the
hands on her watch stood at eight, she lifted the
knocker and gave the door three sharp raps.

Elizabeth didn't know exactly what to expect in response to her knock, but halfway anticipated the door
being opened by either a timid maid dressed in black
and white, a somber-gowned housekeeper with a chain
of keys at her waist, or a dark-clad, stiff-backed but-
ler wearing a disdainful expression.

Instead of her fantasized historical characters, the door swung open to reveal the master of the house, suitably attired in black...not armor, but tight-fitting jeans and a loose, full-sleeved silk shirt. He was barefooted, which should have looked odd, but instead looked both natural and incredibly sexy.

Well, not exactly the run of the mill battle armor, Elizabeth thought, somewhat hysterically. But armor, nonetheless, donned to engage in a subtle sort of attack. A male in soft mail of a sensual difference, designed to breach feminine resistance.

In a word, Lyon looked...devastating.

Elizabeth felt dispirited by the magnetic appeal of him. She had spent an inordinate amount of time dressing for this meeting, eschewing her usual casual, warm weather attire of shorts and pullover for a flower-strewn, full and swirly sheer cotton skirt with a matching low-cut, sleeveless top. She had even gone as far as applying a delicate cover of translucent foundation, eyeliner and shadow, and a swish of color to her cheeks and lips, all in the name of confidence enforcement.

And all to little avail, Elizabeth reflected, suppressing a sigh of discouragement while staring in mute awe at her nemesis. Her efforts and appearance paled into bleak insignificance in comparison to Lyon's dark-garbed, powerful attraction.

Elizabeth was hard put not to babble some excuse, spin on the narrow heel of her white sandals and beat a hasty retreat back to the relative safety of her brother's house.

Too late. The lord of the manor had her pinned to the doorstep with a riveting stare.

"I do admire promptness in a woman," he drawled, pulling the door with him as he stepped back, inviting her inside with a negligent wave of his free hand.

As a greeting, his sexist remark left a lot to be desired and squashed the glimmer of hope Elizabeth was clinging to for their chances of having a civilized discussion.

Tamping down an impulse to deliver a shrill, verbal slap to him, she dredged up a faint smile as she entered the imposing foyer. "Only in a woman?" Elizabeth inquired in a mildly chiding tone. "I find promptness admirable in anyone, male or female."

"Your point," Lyon conceded, giving a slight shrug that set the shimmering silk shirt to rippling sensuously over his shoulders and down his chest.

Oh, help, Elizabeth groaned in silent supplication, giving up her fruitless pretense of interest in the tastefully decorated great hall—which in fact it was, rather than a mere foyer.

Smothering a sigh, she raised her surreptitious gaze from his chest to his eyes, and immediately wished she hadn't. "Is that what this meeting is all about?" she asked, concealing her aroused interest and rising trepidation beneath the cover of sarcasm. "Did you invite—no, order me to come here, for an exercise in scoring points off of each other?"

Lyon's smile was calculated to instill fear into the bravest of souls... of whom Elizabeth did not consider herself a charter member. She felt the fear, and a sense of impending disaster.

"I don't have to indulge myself by scoring points off of you, Elizabeth," he said smoothly. "I am in possession of all the trump cards. Remember?"

The sense of impending disaster ballooned, constricting her breath. "Remember what?" she retaliated, fighting to hang onto her shredding control. "All I've heard were a lot of threats. I've seen no trump cards in the way of proof to back up those threats." She somehow managed a challenging tone and taunting smile. "I think you're running a bluff, Mr. Cantrell."

"Do you?" Lyon's expression hardened into a mask of determination. "Come with me, Ms. Ware," he said, striding across the spacious hall. "I'll be delighted to show you my trump cards of proof."

Up until that moment Elizabeth had only been vaguely aware of the artificial air cooling the huge house. Suddenly, as she followed him to a door at the far end of the hall, she felt the air feather the exposed skin on her arms and shoulders, tracing an icy finger down her spine, chilling her to the bone.

The room Lyon ushered her into was large, dimly lit and even colder than the great hall. Though too riddled with anxiety to notice detail, Elizabeth got an overall impression of gleaming polish on the wooden tables and the large desk near a bank of long windows, thick, plush carpeting, and an abundance of rich supple leather on several deep chairs and a long couch placed at a desk-facing angle in front of a wide fireplace.

Incongruously, a crackling fire leaped in the hearth, ineffectual in combating the chill created by the cool air wafting from the vents leading from the central air-conditioning unit.

"Trump one."

The sharp edge on Lyon's voice jerked Elizabeth's attention away from the room's decor, and her startled gaze to his austere expression. He was holding a folder in one hand, not in offering to her, but more like a prosecutor brandishing an exhibit.

"This is the file on you and your family compiled by the investigative company," he went on when he was satisfied he had her undivided attention. "It is complete, from the day you all pulled up stakes here and disappeared like thieves into the night."

"Thieves? Thieves?" Elizabeth exclaimed, incensed by the insulting term. "How dare—"

"What else?" Lyon interrupted her. "You all vanished without a trace, exactly like a band of hit-and-run outlaws, without a word to anyone, not to friends or neighbors, but especially not to me."

"That's not—" Elizabeth began heatedly.

"You ran away, carrying my child with you," Lyon's harsh voice once again overrode her attempted protest. "Then, to compound your thievery, you denied me my son for nine years and would have continued to do so, probably forever, if I hadn't just happened to see you with him in town three weeks ago."

Elizabeth opened her mouth to refute his accusation, but never got a chance to utter a word.

"Do you have any idea how I felt when I saw him?" Lyon demanded, his growing anger betrayed not only by his tone of voice, though it remained harsh, but by the tautness of tension scoring his features, quivering the length of his muscular frame. "I knew at once that he was mine. Mine, damn you."

Elizabeth was now certain she knew the reason for his sudden interest in Mitch, where he had previously evinced none at all. Jen had told her that he had been married, but that the union had been childless. And now, closing in on forty years of age, Lyon had seen himself reflected in the boy, his near carbon copy. All this—this meeting, his attitude—was about encroaching age, and ego. His ego. She felt sick. Lyon was prepared to destroy his son's life, as well as hers, to insure his own immortality, and to assuage his blasted, arrogant, superior ego.

She was so upset, she could barely articulate. "Damn me?" she cried, clenching her fingers to hide their tremor. "You've got a lot of nerve! You're the one—"

"Yes, damn you," Lyon snarled, again ruthlessly cutting her off. He snatched up another folder from the desktop and took a menacing step toward her. "Ace of trump, honey," he sneered, holding the folder a mere half inch beyond her reach.

"What—" Elizabeth had to pause, to swallow the coppery taste of fear drying her mouth. "What ace?"

"These are faxes of two separate blood studies." Lyon gave her a chilling smile, and set the folder fluttering with a slight flick of his wrist. "The most recent one is mine, of course," he said. "The other is a copy of the one that was done on Mitch soon after he was born in that small hospital in Florida."

Elizabeth experienced a sickening sensation of the floor shifting beneath her feet. Drawing a deep breath, she fought to control the mist of panic beginning to cloud her reasoning faculties.

He was bluffing, she assured herself, frantically grasping at dwindling straws. He had to be bluffing, at least about the copy of Mitch's blood study...not the routine blood-type test, but the work-up done on

Mitch the day before he and Elizabeth were released from the hospital, because the specialist had concerns about jaundice, and something else, which Elizabeth had never really been clear about. Fortunately, the specialist's fears had proved groundless. And, in regard to that study, Elizabeth felt on firmer footing.

Having secured a position in the admissions office in that hospital a few weeks after their arrival in Florida, Elizabeth's own mother had secreted Mitch's records in the hospital computer's confidential files.

Feeling the floor steady somewhat, Elizabeth met Lyon's hard stare with open defiance.

"I still think you're bluffing."

Lyon's smile slid into a mocking curve. "You deny the evidence of your own eyes?"

"I haven't seen anything," she retorted. "If you have anything there, I suspect they are forgeries." She even managed to mirror his mocking smile. "You wave a sheaf of papers in front of my face and expect me to believe they are copies of medical reports that I absolutely know were confidentially sealed?"

Lyon had the unmitigated gall to laugh in her face. "Oh, Elizabeth, how very naive," he chided in condescending tones. "Didn't you know that getting into so-called confidential computer files is merely a challenge to a real computer freak?"

Of course, she knew. Dammit! Elizabeth gritted her teeth in frustration. With all the media coverage on the subject, she couldn't help but know. Still, she refused to concede the point—any point—to him.

She shrugged. It was one of the most difficult actions she had ever contrived. "So you have access to a computer raider. So what? The proof of blood type is hardly irrefutable evidence of paternity."

"Granted," Lyon allowed, with a condescending smile. "But it is enough to convince a hearing judge of the necessity of issuing a court order for more extensive and conclusive tissue testing."

"You would force my son to go through that procedure?" Elizabeth cried, deeply shaken by his threat.

"No, darling," Lyon fairly growled. "If you insist on fighting me, you will be the one forcing *my* son to go through that procedure."

Darling! Anger flared to life inside Elizabeth, lending a strengthening jolt to her fear-weakened spine. She wasn't even sure which of his insults ignited the spark—his use of the endearment, or his claim that, should push come to shove, the blame would be hers. Her sense of outrage nudged her intellect, reminding her of the one and, she prayed, most important trump card she possessed.

"I'm not the brainless fool you obviously believe me to be," she said, somehow managing a confident tone. "I am fully aware of the fact that a judge will rarely rule in favor of removing a child from the natural mother."

"That's true...in most cases," Lyon conceded. "But, then, this isn't most cases."

Elizabeth gave him an arched look. "You don't really believe that an investigative report containing unsubstantiated information about a few late dates is going to convince a judge—any judge—of my lack of moral character, do you?"

"No, I don't. But what I do believe is that money talks," Lyon said with unruffled calm, maddening condescension and a superior smile. "And that big money makes a definite statement."

His pointed barb hit home, deflating Elizabeth's bubble of hope. Desperation rushed in to fill the sudden void. "I'll have my lawyer petition for a staying order," she countered, praying she could find a lawyer both willing and able enough to take on the wealth and power connected to the Cantrell name.

"Be my guest," Lyon invited with infuriating confidence.

"I'll fight you all the way to the supreme court, if I must," Elizabeth promised, growing panicky and overwarm in the too cool air.

"You'll lose." Lyon's smile, his stance, everything about him exuded supreme assurance.

Elizabeth was shaken by an expanding sense of fear that he was right, that she would lose in any contest against the resources at his command. She felt ineffectual, helpless, without recourse. The feelings gave rebirth to outraged anger. Sheer fury rose to mingle with her fear. A lethal combination.

Pushed to the edge of her limits, Elizabeth took a threatening step toward him. "You . . . snake," she hissed from between clenched teeth, throwing caution, and common sense, to the wind. "You son of a—"

"Careful, Elizabeth," Lyon said in cool warning, yet again cutting her off. "I don't suffer fools or insults well. Name calling won't help your cause, and you are already in a precarious position."

In that case . . . Abandoning reason, and all sense of self-preservation, Elizabeth charged at him, hand raised to strike his handsome, sardonic face.

Moving with confusing swiftness, Lyon tossed aside the folder, caught Elizabeth's raised wrist in a steel-fingered grip and, circling her waist with his left arm, hauled her roughly to him, crushing her tender breasts against his hard chest.

"You beast!" Elizabeth exclaimed on the harsh breath expelled from her lungs by the jolting collision of her chest against his.

"Don't expect gentlemanly behavior from me, you little cheat," he growled close to her ear. "Consider yourself fortunate I discarded my first impulse to throttle the deceitful life from your body."

"Me . . . I—I'm deceitful!" Elizabeth sputtered. Incensed beyond endurance, she stiffened her fingers and thrust her arm forward, grazing his hard jaw with the tips of her fingernails.

"You hellcat." White-hot fury blazing from his sapphire eyes, Lyon released her wrist and flung it from him, only to grasp her by the hair. Tangling his fingers in the silky brown strands, he jerked her face to within a whispered breath of his own. "I could beat you senseless. I should beat you senseless," he said in a gritty voice. "But I won't. I am too much of a gentleman to indulge myself with my superior strength."

He loosened his fingers, beginning to untangle them from the rich, dark chocolate-hued mass, when Elizabeth made a fatal blunder.

"Go ahead," she challenged recklessly. "Beat me senseless. Soothe your stupid macho ego by punishing me. Leave bruises and marks on me, a lot of them. Then see how far you get with a custody battle."

Lyon's fingers clenched, tightening, tugging the strands of hair until the sting in her scalp drew a moist sting to her eyes and a gasp to her parted lips.

"You are naive, Elizabeth," he said in a ragged whisper. "Do you honestly believe that I am so unskilled, so inept that I cannot inflict punishment without inflicting bruises and marks on your body?"

Elizabeth's blood ran cold, not from the chilling sound of his voice, or even his threat, but from the sudden change in his eyes. The white-hot fury was gone from their sapphire depths. In its stead simmered a darkening blue haze of sexual arousal.

Elizabeth twisted her head, but she wasn't fast enough. Lyon's mouth took hard possession of hers, crushing her soft lips against her teeth.

He eased the pressure of his hard mouth, and able to breathe once again, Elizabeth inhaled deeply, drawing cool air into her lungs, closing her eyes on a sigh of thankfulness.

Too soon.

Lyon had not finished with his punishment. In fact, he had barely begun. When he resumed his assault, it was with a subtle change of tactic.

"It's been a long time, Elizabeth," he whispered, caressing her smarting lips with a gentle brush of his mouth. "I had almost forgotten the heady taste of your mouth, the exciting feel of your body."

A protest screamed inside Elizabeth's head. Sheer panic tore through her body.

Lyon's mouth brushed hers again, followed by the slick glide of his tongue along the tender inner edge of her throbbing lower lip.

A sob caught, became lodged at the base of her throat. Elizabeth refused to accept the feelings stirring in the most feminine part of her. This couldn't be happening, her mind cried, denying the inner melting sensation. She was no longer eighteen, young, untried, impressionable. This could not be happening to her again. But it was.

Lyon's exquisite application of punishment with his mouth and tongue was making it happen. And, as effortlessly as he had flung her clawing hand from his face, he flung her mind and senses back in time.

Within seconds of his sensual onslaught, Elizabeth was eighteen once more, young, carefree, and in love, eager to experience the right of passage into womanhood by sharing herself, body and soul, with her passionate Lyon.

Her resistance evaporated under the pressurized heat of his hungry mouth. The sob escaped her throat in a low moan as Elizabeth curled her arms around Lyon's taut neck, and met his passion with starving fervor.

Mindless, boneless, lost in a brightly colored, glorious dream of yesteryear, Elizabeth moved when he did, backing up as he stepped forward, not knowing, not caring where Lyon was leading her.

She felt enveloping warmth when he stopped moving and knew they were near the fireplace. Elizabeth didn't care. Her paramount interest lay in the devastating, demoralizing play of his mouth and tongue on her lips, and his hands on her now quivering body.

"You were always so soft," Lyon whispered, abandoning her mouth to explore her face with his lips. "Your skin still feels like warm silk." His hands were beneath her sheer top, gliding it up her body and arms and over her head. The lightweight material fluttered noiselessly to the floor, followed a moment later by her filmy bra. A low groan vibrated in his throat as his hands captured the fullness of her aching breasts.

"God, Elizabeth," he muttered, lowering his tawny head to the scented valley between her breasts. "You *are* more beautiful than before."

Elizabeth didn't comprehend the emphasis he had placed on the present term, but it didn't matter at that moment. What did matter, greatly, were the rioting sensations going berserk inside her.

She was so hot, so hot. Her body was sheened by a dewy film. Her mind was in the process of meltdown.

The distant sound of rumbling thunder played around the edges of her consciousness, making her dimly aware of the growing external atmospheric pressure. Behind her closed eyelids, Elizabeth saw the flash of lightning flickering beyond the long windows, and felt the crackle and sizzle from her nape to the soles of her feet.

Lightning... or the excruciating effects induced by the drawing action of Lyon's mouth on the hard, throbbing tip of her breast?

The whys and wherefores of that didn't matter to Elizabeth, either. She was swirling in a vortex of sensuous memory, light-years removed from reasoning and assimilation of the present.

Feelings, soul-stirring sensations were her realm of the moment. And the terrain of that realm was all-consuming in its erotic splendor.

Responding to the electrifying tug of Lyon's voracious mouth, Elizabeth grasped his head, holding him tightly to her as she arched her back, giving him full access to her breasts. The bowing of her body brought her hips into aligned contact with his, eliciting a groan from Lyon, and a sharp gasp from her in recognition of the magnitude of his arousal.

"Elizabeth." Murmuring her name against her heated flesh, Lyon slid his hands to the waistband of her skirt. His fingers fumbled for an instant, and then the flair of sheer cotton slithered to the floor to form a multi-colored pool around her white sandals. The glide of his palms up the back of her thighs drew a shiver to Elizabeth's limbs and a low purring sound from deep within her throat.

Ten years had passed since Elizabeth had experienced the reckless thrill of intense desire. Except for a few nearly chaste kisses, a few friendly hugs, not since those two joyful weeks with Lyon had she abandoned herself to sensual pleasure. She had held herself aloft, cognizant, thus fearful, of the possible humiliation and shame attendant to shared intimacy.

But this was Lyon. The one and only man ever capable of unleashing the natural sensuality inside her. Yet, even this Lyon was different, more experienced, more mature, infinitely more adept at the art of love-making and sensual arousal.

He whispered words, shocking and exciting, murmured promises of delights in store for both of them, exotic delights, erotic delights. And he acted on those murmured promises with a fluidity and grace that was breathtaking and mind-shattering.

The scrap of silk banding Elizabeth's hips, as well as the black jeans and brief shorts encasing his, disappeared as if by slight of hand.

She felt herself being lowered to the floor and grabbed the front panels of his shirt, which had become undone, seemingly as magically as her panties and his jeans and briefs had disappeared. The silk material caressed the palms of her hands, sending tingling messages up her arms, across her shoulders, and down the length of her now nude torso to the very core of her womanhood.

Elizabeth moaned in response to the sensations, then gasped as the feelings were intensified by the sudden soft abrasion of the carpet fibers against her bare back.

"A male fantasy come true," Lyon murmured, skimming his mouth down the arched curve of her throat. "A beautiful, desirable woman, stretched out in mindless abandonment beneath him on the floor next to a raging fire."

At any other time Elizabeth would have taken exception to his remark, considering it chauvinistic in content, insulting in its impersonal meaning.

But this wasn't any other time. This was here and now, and Lyon's kisses, his caresses, his laving tongue were driving her to the very edge of sanity, exacerbating her excitement, even as the proof of his own sizzling excitement was made evident to her.

Instead of voicing a protest, going stiff with resentment, Elizabeth made a murmuring sound of heightened excitement, and moved sinuously in response to the fiery trail of his mouth down the length of her body from her arched neck to her slender ankles.

She was writhing, burning in the blaze of passion, by the time Lyon's greedy mouth retraced the trail of scorching kisses. No longer aware of what she was doing, she scraped the black silk shirt from his shoulders and back, needing the tactile sensation of her hands on his smooth, hot skin.

His chest settled on her breasts, the golden whorls of wiry hair a rough enticement to madness against the tight tips of her aching breasts.

"I can't bear it," Lyon said in a ragged mutter, gliding his hands down her torso to separate her thighs. "I want this to last forever," he went on in a desperate whisper, drawing a shattered groan from Elizabeth when his fingers found the core of her dementia.

Beyond speaking, a ten-year need lashing her on, Elizabeth's body jerked, arching high in a mute appeal, demand, to be joined with his.

"Elizabeth!" Lyon exclaimed through clenched teeth. "I can't wait . . . I . . ." He thrust into her, shuddered, then became still, as if savoring the homecoming.

Elizabeth was having none of his hesitancy. Whipped into a frenzy of need by the intensity of his advance, she grasped his taut buttocks and, arching even higher, glided her body back and forth against the fullness of his hard, throbbing arousal.

Lyon groaned a curse against her lips, then thrust his tongue into her mouth, repeatedly, moving it in and out in time with the deep thrusts of his quivering body.

Tension coiled ever higher inside Elizabeth, tightening, tightening until she feared she would scream aloud with her need for release. Her fingers clenched, digging mercilessly into the rock-hard muscles of Lyon's buttocks. Her mouth drank greedily from his, as her tongue engaged his in an erotic duel. Her body moved, arching higher, and yet higher, seeking, seeking the ultimate goal.

But Lyon was in supreme command, and obviously determined to draw out the moment, and excruciating pleasure, to the nth degree. Again and again, his timing perfect, he brought her to the very edge of infinity, only to withdraw, denying her completion, heightening her now raging desire.

Sobbing, Elizabeth demanded, then begged him to set her free of this terrible, unbearable, delicious sensation of sensuality.

And still, Lyon refused, driving himself and her to the outer limits of control.

And then his control snapped. With a garbled mutter growling in his throat, he bore down on her, thrusting, grinding into her until, finally, she did scream aloud in the throes of her release. An instant later Lyon's own harsh grunt of fulfillment echoed on the cool air in the silent room.

Elizabeth was free. Free. Her mind couldn't bear the shattering power and all-encompassing immensity of it, and so escaped beneath the tranquilizing black blanket of unconsciousness.

Elizabeth had no idea exactly how long she lay senseless and insensitive to her surroundings. It could have been a few seconds or a few hours. But, when she awoke, it was to complete clarity of mind...and mental anguish.

Lyon slept the deep sleep of physical repletion beside her, his beautiful, muscularly trim body sprawled in a pose of utter relaxation.

Beginning to shake with remorse for her self-betrayal, Elizabeth averted her gaze from the too enticing sight of his supine form, and eased away from the too beguiling contact with his warm flesh.

Staring with haunted eyes at the flames now flickering low on the hearth, she pulled on her clothes, stepped into her sandals and made a beeline for the door, snatching up her handbag from the floor as she fled from the room, through the great hall, out the front door, and into a wild and wind-tossed thunderstorm.

Elizabeth was soaked to the skin before she had descended the three smoothed stone steps to the driveway. The pounding rain felt like chips of ice pelting her passion-flushed body. Shivering in reaction to the sudden chill, of flesh and sensibilities, she dashed for the car, stabbed the key into the ignition and fired the engine. Then, her vision blurred by the tears flooding her eyes, pouring down her face, she tore away from the looming house like a bat out of hell.

She had gone no more than several hundred yards from the entranceway to Lyon's house when she was forced to pull off to the side of the sharply curving road. The sheeting rain and her own tears made visibility impossible. Shaking uncontrollably from reaction, Elizabeth crumpled against the steering wheel and gave way to the racking sobs tearing at her chest.

Betrayal. Betrayal. Betrayal.

The condemnation beat incessantly inside her mind in time with the streaking lightning and booming thunder. For an instant's pleasure, a moment to relive the dream that had haunted her for ten long, empty years, she had betrayed herself, but infinitely more shocking and condemning was the realization that she had betrayed her precious son, as well.

How could she, how could she have committed such an unspeakable act? she railed at herself, gagging and choking on her tears.

If only she could place the blame entirely on Lyon, accuse him of taking her against her will, in an arrogant variation of droit du seigneur.

But she couldn't, Elizabeth acknowledged, sniffling. She was too honest, and though it was true that Lyon had initially forced the situation, honesty demanded she accept her share of responsibility, if only for her lapse of moral strength and fiber.

The self-damning truth was that, other than her single weak-willed no at the outset, she had put forth no real effort to repulse him.

As unpalatable as it was to accept, Elizabeth knew that she was as guilty as Lyon. The truth was as agonizing as a blade thrust to her breast, but there it was.

Elizabeth felt certain she had sunk to the very depths of degradation and torment, and then another, still more horrifying realization struck her, wrenching a cry of protest to her seared throat.

Her downfall had not been caused by mere chance, nor by the magnetic tug of blind physical attraction, nor the mind-destroying sight, feel and touch of him.

Maybe she was still in love with Lyon!

In that instant of blinding admission, Elizabeth had the answer to the question that had nagged at her during the anxiety-ridden drive to his house.

She *was* out of her mind.

Five

Elizabeth was gone.

Lyon knew before he opened his eyes that she was no longer lying beside him. He felt it, instinctively, deep down, in his bones, in his gut.

A broken sigh whispered through his parched lips, a sigh of regret, a sigh of unbelievable emptiness and, to his amazement, a sigh of remorse.

"Dammit," he muttered, jackknifing into a sitting position.

"Elizabeth." Her name escaped his throat, his guard, his rigid control.

Why had he touched her? Lyon upbraided himself, staring into the dying fire. Elizabeth had cheated him out of nine years of his son's life, he reminded himself, shoving the sense of remorse into the depths of his subconscious. She deserved any form of retribution he meted out to her. *He* was holding all the cards, the power to destroy her. When and why had he lost sight of his objective? What demon of lust had inspired him to lay hands on her?

Lust. Lyon's harsh groan quivered in the silent room. Lord, had he ever before felt such an agony of lust? he reflected, knowing he had not. The need to touch Elizabeth, taste her, be one with her, had consumed him, mind, body and soul.

An intense shiver washed over his body.

Shifting his bleak gaze from the fireplace, Lyon observed the tiny goose bumps covering his arms and torso, and the evidence of immediate quickening to his manhood, fully aware the physical reaction had been caused by an inner response to the memory of the encounter with Elizabeth.

He wanted her again, needed her again, as desperately as he had wanted, needed her . . . when, an hour, two hours ago? Lyon shook his head. The passage of time held no meaning. He wanted her, wanted her, every bit as much as he had wanted her ten years ago.

"No." Lyon shook his head, as if trying to clear his mind and senses of the effects from a strong physical blow. No, he did not want her as much as he had ten years ago; he wanted her more, infinitely more.

Why? The self-query startled him; the answer, not fully formed but shocking in its shadowy intent, startled him even more.

Growing still, barely breathing, Lyon listened, not to his incoherent thoughts, but to the silent inner messages being relayed to him from his emotions.

"No." A whisper. A groan. A plea of denial.

Still the messages continued to tap against the closed door of his consciousness.

"No." Stronger now, the denial made an impression in the noiseless room.

The messages persisted.

"No!" Lyon barked, his eyes blazing angry defiance of the inner emotional upheaval. "I am not in love with her again. I will not allow it. It's lust. Physical. Chemistry. Nothing more..." His voice lost strength, dwindling to a husky murmur. "I can't go through that again."

At that moment Lyon's mind reasserted itself, rescuing him by reviving memory—recent memory. The scene swirled in living color before his inner eye. Elizabeth lay stretched out on the carpet, her skin flushed by passion, her moist lips parted, her arms raised to enfold a lover, her body arched in a pose of utter abandonment, revealing the lust of an experienced woman.

Lust. Yes, Lyon assured himself. Elizabeth lusted for him, even as he had lusted for her.

Relief quaking through him, cold and hot at the same time, Lyon reached for his clothes. After shrugging into his shirt, he stood and stepped into the now wrinkled jeans. A belated realization slammed into him as he carefully guided the zipper up and over his aroused flesh.

He had failed to protect Elizabeth and himself against the possible procreative results of his mindless action.

Lyon froze in place, hands falling limply to his sides, leaving the top snap on his jeans undone. But, while his body stilled, his mind raced forward.

What if he had once again planted his seed in the fertile cradle of Elizabeth's womb?

Lyon was shaken to his depths by a streaking thrill of emotion in reaction to the speculative thought. Yet, strangely, the thrill was one of anticipation, not, as he would have expected, consternation.

Anticipation? Lyon repeated the word in silent wonder, testing it, and himself. Why anticipation? he probed, carefully, fearfully, delving into the murky areas of his rattled mind.

Because then you could have her, force her to accept you... on a permanent basis, the answer sprang forth, stark and full-blown.

Marriage? Lyon mused, sending another probe into the inexplicable workings of his mental morass.

What else? the morass shot back.

Along with a shiver feathering the surface of his skin, Lyon was now treated to a film of perspiration sheening his forehead and upper lip.

"Are you nuts?"

You want her, don't you?

"Yes... but... marriage?"

Why not? It is binding... somewhat.

"But she cheated me, ran away from me before. I'd have to be altogether out of my mind to even consider tying myself to her, giving my name to her."

Lyon flinched, startled by the harsh sound of his own voice. Damned if he wasn't talking to himself... talking, hell, he was arguing with himself!

You'd also be giving your name to your son, and possible future offspring, the inner voice of consciousness pointed out with cool reason.

Future offspring. Lyon rolled the concept around in his head, silently this time.

In addition to Elizabeth in your bed at night, every night, instead of on the floor.

Lyon's throat worked in a hard, painful swallow. Lowering his gaze to the floor, he once again, this time deliberately, envisioned Elizabeth there, eager and passionate, ready and willing, waiting for him. In retrospect, having her there, on the floor, had been pretty damned exciting.

His shiver expanded into a body-racking shudder of intensified need for her.

Face it, Cantrell, you want her so bad your teeth hurt, you've wanted her since the day of her eighteenth birthday party, the imp of the inner voice chided.

Yes, Lyon confessed in mute defeat.

So, get her, whether or not you've planted your seed this time, go get her, the voice came back, cold and ruthless.

Yes. Lyon raised his head in male arrogance. The dying embers in the fireplace reflected the shimmering gleam of calculation in the sapphire depths of his eyes. He was in possession of the means to bend her to his will . . . with or without the necessity of marriage.

One way or another, Lyon vowed, whether for revenge or pure physical necessity, he would obtain complete control of Elizabeth.

The rain had diminished into a steady downpour by the time Elizabeth had regained enough of her control to resume driving.

A groan swelled in her throat and escaped as she pulled into the driveway of her brother's house. Lights blazed from the living-room windows, a clear indication to Elizabeth that Jen was waiting up for her, waiting and very likely itching for an in-depth postmortem of Elizabeth's meeting with Lyon, the scourge of the mountain.

Elizabeth sighed. The last thing she wanted to do was talk about their confrontation. Talk about it? She didn't want to think about it.

Elizabeth was wet, and she was chilled, and she was to-the-soul tired. Heaving another sigh, she shoved the door open and dragged her aching and depleted body from the car. She didn't even bother to dash for the protective roof over the front door; she was already soaked, how much wetter could she get?

"Good heavens!" Jen exclaimed at the sight of Elizabeth sloshing into the house. "Didn't you have an umbrella with you in the car?"

Elizabeth frowned. An umbrella? Come to think of it, she did keep one in the car, for just such occasions as this. She simply hadn't thought of it, and admitted as much. "Yes, but I forgot it," she replied, deliberately omitting the information that remembering wouldn't have done her much good, anyway, since she'd received the drenching while dashing from Lyon's house to the car.

Jen rolled her eyes. "You're a mess."

Tell me about it.

Keeping the retort to herself, Elizabeth nodded in agreement. "I know. It was really coming down for a while there," she went on. "I had to pull over because I couldn't see the road."

"Poor thing," Jen commiserated. "You go right up and get out of those wet clothes," she instructed, turning to head for the kitchen. "I'll make a cup of hot tea for you . . . and lace it with whiskey."

"Sounds heavenly," Elizabeth said, squashing an impulse to add, *but leave out the tea.*

Fifteen minutes and a hot shower later, Elizabeth entered the kitchen, her body wrapped in a mid-calf length terry-cloth robe and her dripping hair swathed in a large bath towel.

"Better?" Jen asked, turning from the sink to place a steaming cup on the Formica-topped table.

"Yes." Elizabeth dropped like a stone onto a chair, curled her cold hands around the warm cup and offered her friend a weak smile. "Thanks."

"It was bad, huh?"

Elizabeth was stuck for a reply, since two entirely different answers simultaneously sprang into her mind, the first being, *it was awful,* the second being, *it was wonderful.* Immediately rejecting the wonderful part, she opted for the awful.

"Yes."

"Well?" Jen frowned. "Tell me."

"In a nutshell, he's not bluffing." Cradling the cup, Elizabeth raised it to her lips for a tentative sip, hoping the hot, laced tea would ease the tight achy feeling gripping her throat.

Jen's frown gave way to an expression of utter bafflement. "But, I don't understand. He was at fault here. What proof could he possibly have?"

Speaking in a dull, metronomic tone, Elizabeth related to Jen the facts of Lyon's "trump cards," ending with his intimations of that afternoon. "And, as the investigative report contained exact places, times and the names of every man I've dated over the past ten years, Lyon has concluded that I am immoral and promiscuous, thus not a fit mother for *his* son."

"Immoral! Promiscuous! You?" Jen exclaimed, bursting into incredulous laughter. "That's the most ludicrous thing I have ever heard. Why, you're the most straight-laced, twentieth-century woman I know."

"Yes, well." Elizabeth moved her shoulders in a feeble, defeated-looking shrug. "Since some of those dates ended up rather late in my apartment, and there were no witnesses to claim otherwise, Lyon insinuated that I was cavorting with my male companions while Mitch innocently slept in the next room."

"I don't believe this!" Jen looked flabbergasted. "As if you, of all people, would ever dream of allowing yourself to be swept away by any man!"

Elizabeth concealed an involuntary wince behind the cup. Cringing inside, she faced the damning truth that she had allowed herself to be swept away by a man. The fact that the man was not merely the only man she had ever loved, but her son's father, as well, didn't excuse her rash and unforgivable behavior. She was guilty as sin, and she knew it. Elizabeth accepted the guilt without question.

"But Lyon doesn't know that," she said, rubbing her tired, tear-stung eyes. "What he does know is that I was once swept away by one man—him."

"And so it follows that you'd be willing to jump into the sack with any man," Jen concluded. "Typical." Her lips tightened, then she smiled. "But Lyon is forgetting one important fact here."

"And that is?" Elizabeth asked, hoping her friend had thought of something, some lever she, in her state of confusion, had overlooked.

"A judge rarely rules against the mother."

Elizabeth's hope and spirits took a nosedive. "I pointed that out to Lyon."

"And?" Jen prompted, her smile fading at the sound of defeat in Elizabeth's voice.

"He pointed a more realistic factor out to me. That money talks and big money talks even louder... or words to that effect."

"You need a lawyer." Jen's decisive voice pierced the memory clouding Elizabeth's mind.

"I know."

"Damn, I wish Chuck was here."

Elizabeth sighed. "Not nearly as much as I do. I haven't the vaguest idea who to call." Her growing weariness was reflected in the quiver in her voice. "All I do know is that I need a really good lawyer, one willing to stand up to the Cantrell name, and the power it entails."

The normally feisty Jen swallowed, betraying a surfacing sense of uneasiness. "Kinda daunting, isn't it."

"No," Elizabeth said, feeling her own fears expanding. "It's terrifying."

It wasn't until later, in the privacy of her room, while drying her still damp hair, that the realization of her vulnerability slammed into Elizabeth.

What if she had conceived?

Elizabeth was so shaken by the thought, the possibility, that the blow-dryer dropped from her trembling fingers, landing with a thump on the dresser surface.

Staring dully at the humming appliance, she frantically assured herself that it couldn't happen.

Could it?

Elizabeth's thoughts fractured, scurrying in several different directions at once, none of them logical, reasonable or rational.

What was the old saw . . . it only took one time?

It had happened before.

But not on the first time!

Another child . . . without a visible father?

Perhaps a girl this time.

No!

Elizabeth shuddered and enforced control over her rioting thoughts, not from despair or even fear, but because of the leap of excitement generated deep down inside her by the improbable prospect of nurturing the seed of Lyon's daughter.

No, no and no. Even as she repeated the denial, Elizabeth envisioned the female counterpart of Mitch, blond, blue-eyed, beautiful.

"No." A whisper of regret, but a whisper of strength. Her mind now clear, Elizabeth calculated the days of the month, concluding that the chances of her having conceived this unreal night were slim to none.

Reaching out with fingers now cold but steady, Elizabeth switched off the blow-dryer. A moment later she switched off the bedside lamp, seeking release from worry and confusion in the soothing arms of oblivion.

Two, then three, then four long, harrowing days passed without a word of communication from Lyon. Throughout every one of those endless days, Elizabeth swung between the emotional extremes of hope and despair.

Taking the initiative, Jen had placed an overseas call to Chuck the morning after Elizabeth's meeting with Lyon. While viciously cursing the Cantrell name, and his inability to desert his post to rush back to the States to support his sister, Chuck produced the name of a very prestigious, and very expensive, Philadelphia law firm, along with a promise to not only arrange an appointment for Elizabeth, but to assume the legal fees, as well.

Hope was born inside Elizabeth after her first telephone conversation with a senior member of the law firm, a confident-sounding Mr. Mendelson who, upon hearing the particulars of her case, assured her that he would do everything legally possible to defend her right to custody of her child, beginning with his own investigation of the facts surrounding the case.

Before disconnecting, Elizabeth set up an appointment to meet with Mr. Mendelson in his office soon after her return to the Philadelphia area.

Despair encroached with the closing of each successive day without a word or message from Lyon.

There were only a few days left of Elizabeth's vacation. She was scheduled for a flight to Phoenix from her base at Philadelphia International two days after her return home. She could not delay her departure.

Nevertheless, Elizabeth put off packing, waiting, waiting for the phone to ring, or the sight of Lyon's sports car pulling into the driveway.

What was he up to?

Speculation tormented Elizabeth incessantly. By the fifth day, she felt as if she were walking blindfolded through a booby-trapped maze, a maze, moreover, of her own construction.

In addition to the constant uncertainty about Lyon's machinations, Elizabeth questioned her own moral fiber. What flaw or quirk existed inside her, what weakness of character did she possess that left her quivering at the memory of Lyon's lovemaking?

Elizabeth considered herself a strong, intelligent woman. And yet, the sight, the sound, of Lyon, the merest touch from him, had always had the power to reduce her to a quivering mass of emotions and sensations.

She had loved him once with every particle of her being. *Had* that love been strong enough, deep enough to survive his cruel and unforgivable rejection?

Or was she simply grasping for an excuse for her own unforgivable surrender to sensuality?

And what about Lyon? Elizabeth further questioned. He had not taken her that night, he had made love to her. What had motivated him?

He had threatened to take her child from her. Would Lyon go through with it? Could he go through with it?

Questions, questions, hammering inside Elizabeth's head, making her fearful and furious in turn. As each day crept by, she became more quiet, withdrawn, jumpy. Jen observed her with watchful, compassion-filled eyes. Mitch gave her leery looks and a wide berth. Teetering on an emotional precipice, she put off packing until late in the afternoon of the last day.

"I feel as though I should be doing something," she said, suppressing an urge to ball the blouse in her hands and toss it into the open suitcase on the bed.

"You are doing something," Jen said. "You're finally packing to go home."

Elizabeth shifted her gaze from the garment she was carefully folding to give her sister-in-law a wry smile. "That isn't what I mean and you know it."

"Yes, I know." Jen slipped another blouse from a hanger and began folding it. "You feel the need for action."

"Yes." Heaving a sigh, Elizabeth took the blouse from Jen and placed it in the case. "This uncertainty is driving me crazy."

Jen responded with an arched look and a pointed query. "You think Lyon doesn't know what his silent game of cat and mouse is doing to you?"

"Oh, he knows," Elizabeth muttered, flinging the neatly folded blouse into the case. "In fact, I'd bet he's banking on it."

"Maybe some action is called for," Jen mused, narrowing her eyes in a sly manner.

"Like what?" Elizabeth prompted hesitantly, familiar, thus wary of her friend's crafty expression.

"Well, you could drive up the mountain to that fortress, and when Lyon answers the door, give vent to your anger and frustration with a hard right to his breadbasket."

Jen's obvious purpose was achieved. For the first time in days, Elizabeth laughed, spontaneously and without strain. She was still laughing, envisioning herself acting on Jen's suggestion, when the sound of Mitch's raised voice carried to her from the base of the stairway.

"Hey, Mom! Mr. Cantrell's at the door, says he wants to see you."

Elizabeth's laughter died a choking death in her throat, and she stared at Jen in wide-eyed apprehension. "Wh-what do you suppose he wants?" she whispered, as if afraid Lyon could overhear her.

"Probably to twist the knife with more of his threats," Jen muttered in tones of disgust. "Why don't you go down there and tell him to take a high-flying leap off the battlements of his damned fortress?"

This time Jen's purpose fell flat; Elizabeth could dredge up little more than a weak smile in response. She felt sick with fear, yet strangely excited by the prospect of tangling with Lyon again. She wanted to run and hide, and run to meet him, at one and the same time. The inner conflict kept her motionless, speechless.

"Mom?" Mitch yelled.

Elizabeth stared at the open doorway.

Jen answered for her. "Tell him to come in, Mitch. Your mother will be right down."

Elizabeth was bombarded by flashing memories, not of the pain inflicted upon her by Lyon's cavalier treatment of her, but of his hungry mouth, his searching hands, his taut, hard body. She wet her lips, swallowed, and ran her tongue over her fear-dried lips once more. She couldn't, she just could not face him, not this soon after her shaming surrender. But Elizabeth also knew she couldn't tell Jen that, couldn't explain.

"I—I don't want to talk to him. I'll let my lawyer do my talking for me," she said, her voice raw, her eyes beseeching understanding from Jen. "Please, Jen, you go down, tell him to go away."

Jen stared at her in blank astonishment. "You're afraid of him? You, the woman I always believed was not afraid of anything or anybody?"

"Don't you understand?" Elizabeth cried, then, glancing at the open door, moved to shut it and give herself a few precious seconds to come up with a plausible reason. "This isn't anything or anybody. This is the powerful Lyon Cantrell, and he has initiated legal action to take Mitch away from me." She paused to draw a deep breath, in hopes of calming her racing thoughts and smothering a traitorous, insidious tight coil of sensual excitement unwinding inside her.

"No, I don't understand," Jen spoke in that moment of calm-gathering silence. "You've been going
bananas all week, wondering what he is planning.
Well, here's your chance to find out." She shrugged.
"Who knows, you might even be able to taunt some
useful information out of him, some ammunition for
your lawyer to use in the upcoming custody battle."

"Maybe," Elizabeth conceded, recognizing good
on-the-spot strategy—when it was laid out for her.
"But I don't know if I can—"

"Besides," Jen cut in, delivering the coup de grace,
"I'd think the absolute last thing you'd want is for
Lyon to get the notion that you're afraid of him."

Innate pride rushed to the fore to resolve Elizabeth's indecisiveness. Pride and an innocent if goad-
ing call from her son.

"Hey, Mom? Lyon said to tell you he's getting tired
of cooling his heels down here—whatever that
means—and if you don't come down, he'll come up
there."

Lyon said what?

Lyon!

Elizabeth whipped around to glare at the door. So
he had instructed Mitch to call him Lyon, had he?
Renewed, courage-bolstering anger sizzled through
her. Well, she'd see about that, she fumed, striding to
the door. She'd also see if she could wrangle some information out of the so-assured, ego-inflated Lyon

Cantrell. Invade her bedroom, would he? Elizabeth railed as she descended the stairs. She'd see about that, as well.

She could only pray that Mr. Mendelson possessed the legal expertise and adroitness to apply whatever bits of gold she might mine from the rock-hard, granite-faced man waiting for her.

Apparently deserted by Mitch, Lyon stood alone and at his ease in front of the wide window, looking too confident, too sophisticated, too imperious in the small, homey, country-style decor of Jen's living room.

Unaware and unconcerned with the fiery challenge blazing from her anger-darkened brown eyes, or the silky strands of equally dark hair flying around her squared shoulders, Elizabeth swept into the room, fixed a drilling stare on the scion of the Cantrell family, and drew a deep breath, preparing to launch a verbal attack.

"Just who in the hell do you think you are?"

Though obviously caught off-guard by the suddenness of her offensive, Lyon rallied swiftly, responding with a cool counteroffensive. "I know exactly who I am. I am Mitchell's father." His quick, feral smile conveyed blatant self-assurance. "I am also the man calling the shots in this situation."

"Really?" Elizabeth taunted thinking—hoping—his overripe ego might be ready for harvesting. "Aren't you jumping to optimistic conclusions?"

"I don't think so," Lyon said, his smile reflecting her taunting tone.

An uncomfortable sensation of intuition, premonition—something scary—invaded Elizabeth's stomach. Hanging onto her facade of composure, she worked her mouth into an unperturbed smile. "At the risk of raining on your little parade, I feel I must remind you of the fact that a court hearing hasn't even been scheduled as yet."

"True," he conceded too readily.

The gut feeling of impending disaster expanded inside Elizabeth. Needing answers, more for herself now than as ammunition for Mr. Mendelson, she faced him with open defiance. "What arrogant notion would lead you to believe that you're calling the shots?"

"The simple fact that my lawyers have already had several promising conferences with the judge chosen to hear my petition." Lyon's tone and smile were loaded with self-confidence and satisfaction.

"That's not ethical!" Elizabeth exclaimed in shocked protest.

"Why isn't it?" he retorted. "If you'll recall, I did tell you that the petition was filed weeks ago. The judge only agreed to confer with my lawyers when you didn't respond with a counter suit."

"But I wasn't even notified!"

"Wrong," Lyon said. "An effort was made to inform you of the instigation of legal action."

"But I wasn't at home, I was here," Elizabeth cried. "And you knew it."

"Yes, I knew, but there's no law that I'm aware of stating that I must reveal everything I know." He shrugged. "I merely chose to keep the information to myself."

"You did it deliberately, to undermine my position," Elizabeth lashed out at him.

"Of course," he admitted. "I fully intend to win my custody suit and, from the information I received a few hours ago from my lawyers, all indications are that I'm going to win."

Mitch! She was going to lose him! Panic gripped Elizabeth, urging her to find her son and run with him, in a manner similar to the way her own parents had run away with her ten years ago. Her thoughts darted in different directions, searching for a means of escape, a place of refuge.

"I have a proposition for you." Lyon's incisive tone sliced through the fog of panic clouding Elizabeth's mind, snaring her attention. "If you're willing, you could end this litigation here and now."

"A proposition?" Elizabeth asked warily. "What sort of proposition?"

"You can keep your son, on one condition."

Elizabeth knew she wasn't going to like his condition. And yet she was ready to agree to almost anything to keep Mitch with her. She hesitated an instant, fearful and uncertain, then she drew a deep breath and threw caution to the wind.

"Name it."

"Come live with me, and bring Mitch with you."

Six

"**W**hat?" Elizabeth stared at Lyon in astonishment, then gave a gurgle of incredulous laughter. This turn of events was beyond belief! Lyon was asking her to come live with him? No, he wasn't asking, he was demanding she come live with him.

It was too much...way too much for Elizabeth to contend with. Ten years ago, when she would have joyfully followed him to the edge—and over—any precipice, Lyon had spurned her love, rejected her and their unborn child with cold, impersonal arrogance.

Now, after ten years of hating and longing for him in turn, ten years of bitterness and regret, Lyon had the unmitigated gall to issue ultimatums?

From a distance, Elizabeth heard the trill summons of a ringing phone, but the sound didn't register on her whirling thoughts. She must have misunderstood. Yes, that was it. Surely he hadn't said what she thought she had heard him say? No, he couldn't have...

"You heard correctly," Lyon said, almost as if he could read her fractured mind.

"Come live with you?" she said, shaking her head in disbelief. "Are you out of your thick—"

"Ah...excuse me," Jen inserted from where she stood, hovering in the kitchen archway.

"—little skull?" Elizabeth finished, barely noticing her friend's attempt to catch her attention.

"No, I'm offering you a bargain," Lyon replied, turning to give Jen a repressive stare.

"I'm really sorry to interrupt, but—" Jen tried again, ignoring Lyon's fierce scowl.

"Bargain?" Elizabeth exclaimed, once more cutting off her friend. "That's not a bargain, it's out and out blackmail!"

"Call it what you like, but—"

"Elizabeth!"

"Dammit, woman," Lyon snapped, glaring at Jen. "Can't whatever it is wait?"

Lyon's harsh tone accomplished what Jen's anxious voice had failed to do. Before the momentarily speechless Jen had a chance to snap back at him, Elizabeth rushed into the breach. "What is it, Jen?"

"The phone," Jen bit out, casting a seething look at Lyon. "You're wanted on the phone."

Lyon made a rude noise of exasperation. "Why don't you take a message?"

Jen thrust her small chin out belligerently. "Why don't you take a hike?"

"Jen, please, take a message," Elizabeth said, exhaling a tired sigh. "I can't talk now, I'll have to return the call later."

"I think you'd better take it now," Jen advised. "It's Mr. Mendelson."

"Who the devil is—" Lyon began.

Elizabeth wasn't listening. Turning away, she dashed for the kitchen, her thoughts racing ahead of her. Maybe Mr. Mendelson had some good news for her, a reprieve from this unbelievable situation. She fervently hoped so, for unless he had found some way to block Lyon's steam-roller action, she didn't know what she would or could do.

Saying a silent prayer, Elizabeth drew a quick breath and picked up the receiver. Deep inside, with absolute certainty, she knew that she could and would do anything to keep her son, even if that anything meant compliance with Lyon's outlandish proposition.

"Hello, Mr. Mendelson?" she said in a voice raw with anxiety. "This is Elizabeth Ware."

"I'm afraid I have some unsettling news for you, Ms. Ware," the lawyer responded without preamble, sending her hopes and spirits plummeting.

All the energy seemed to drain from Elizabeth's body, leaving her feeling weak, riddled with trepidation. Closing her eyes, she leaned forward and rested her forehead against the cool surface of the smooth, painted kitchen wall.

"Ms. Ware?"

"I'm still here," she answered.

"Are you all right?" he asked, obviously concerned. "Your voice sounds strange."

"I'm fine," she lied. "Please, go on."

"Yes, well . . ." Mr. Mendelson paused to clear his throat, as if hesitant to continue, then he said briskly, "I have just received the findings of the investigative report on the information which you supplied to me earlier this week, and it would appear that there are no facts to corroborate your story."

Elizabeth's eyes flew open and she pushed away from the wall, stiff with shock. "What? Are you calling me a liar, Mr. Mendelson?"

"No, no, of course not," he replied at once in soothing tones. "Please, understand, I am simply stating the results of the investigation."

"But I don't understand," Elizabeth cried. "Every word I told you was the truth."

"I have no doubts about your veracity," the lawyer assured her. "What I am saying is that there are no facts of record to support your story."

"No facts of record?" Elizabeth repeated, dazed. "What does that mean?"

"It means we have no concrete, substantiating proof to present to the hearing judge."

"But what about the payoff check Mr. Cantrell gave to my father?" she demanded, her voice unsteady, reedy with desperation. "There must be a record of a check for that exorbitant amount of money."

"That's correct, there is a record of the check, endorsed by your father," the lawyer confirmed.

"But, then . . ." Elizabeth began.

"Please, let me finish, Ms. Ware." Mr. Mendelson's deep voice overshadowed hers. "The fact that your father endorsed the check means nothing in this instance, since the check had not been signed by either the elder or the younger Mr. Cantrell."

"What?" Elizabeth's mind reeled. "I don't understand," she repeated, numbed. "How could that be?"

"Had you ever examined the check?"

"No, as I told you when we spoke before, I didn't want to accept the check. I never even looked at it. I didn't want anything to do with their buy-off money."

"Quite understandable, under the circumstances," Mr. Mendelson intoned. "But, had you examined the check, you might possibly have noticed some factors which now, ten years later, are of paramount importance.'' He paused to draw a breath, then proceeded to send her hopes crashing. "You see, Ms. Ware, your father didn't cash the check until after your family had resettled in Florida, simply because the check was postdated.''

Elizabeth blinked, and blurted out, "I'm getting more confused by the minute. What does the date on the check or when my father cashed it have to do with it?''

"I'll explain,'' he said with infinite patience. "But first, you did tell me your father was employed as a foreman for a local shoe factory, didn't you?''

"Yes,'' she replied, becoming even more confused. "But what has that—''

"The shoe factory's records show that your father's stated reason for leaving the company was for personal advancement.''

"But that was just an excuse,'' she inserted.

"Undoubtedly,'' Mr. Mendelson replied. "But, unfortunately, the check he subsequently cashed was drawn on the account of a small shoe factory in Ohio, in payment to your father for consultant services. The check was signed by the treasurer of the company, which, by the way, is now defunct.''

Elizabeth's lips flattened into a grim line of acceptance. She might be confused, but she wasn't stupid.

She didn't require elaboration; she got the picture. But she did have one more question.

"Tell me, Mr. Mendelson, did your investigation ascertain whether or not the Ohio company was part of the Cantrell conglomeration?"

"Yes, of course, at one time it was," he confirmed her suspicion. "But, since the Cantrell group sold the Ohio firm just prior to the date your father cashed the check, I'm sorry to say the judge considers the information insufficient to indicate bribery."

"But my mother and father can give testimony, explain the circumstances of Mr. Cantrell's visit to our home, and how he made his generous offer—in Lyon's name!" Elizabeth exclaimed, clutching at straws.

"I've considered that possibility, Ms. Ware," he said, warning her of what was to follow by heaving a regretful-sounding sigh. "As a matter of fact, I have already contacted your parents about giving depositions. But I feel duty bound to caution you not to get your hopes up in that respect, simply because the elder Mr. Cantrell is no longer available to either confess to or contest the validity of their testimony."

"Yes, I see," she said in a tone of utter defeat. "We've lost, haven't we? Even before ever getting to the hearing, we've lost."

"Naturally I will continue to pursue every avenue in your defense," Mr. Mendelson said. "But in all honesty, I must admit that at this point..."

His voice trailed away, taking the last of her hope of victory with it.

After disconnecting, Elizabeth stood, head bowed, shoulders slumped, her hand still clutching the receiver.

Mother. She had to talk to her mother.

Her lips trembling, tears gathering to burn her eyes, Elizabeth lifted the receiver. She began dialing, then her fingers fell away from the buttons and landed on the disconnect bar.

What could she say? "Hi, Mother, how's Dad? Help me, I'm losing my son, and you might lose your grandson." No. Elizabeth cradled the receiver. She couldn't do that to her parents. Her father had suffered a stroke just a year ago, she couldn't dump her own fears—

"Elizabeth?" Jen's concerned-sounding voice broke into Elizabeth's reverie. "Honey, what is it? What did Mr. Mendelson say? You look like death."

And I feel worse. Elizabeth kept the response to herself; deciding she had dumped enough of her problems on Jen, too. Raising her head, she squared her shoulders and drew a deep breath.

"I'm okay," she said, giving Jen a shaky smile. "I . . . If you don't mind, I need some time alone with Lyon." She held up her hand when her sister-in-law got a familiar bullish look and opened her mouth to object. "There are some, er, things we need to work out."

Jen looked unconvinced and on the point of argument. Elizabeth forestalled her.

"I'll be all right. Honestly," she said, her smile tilting at a wry angle. "I assure you, Lyon won't gobble me up or anything."

"I wouldn't bank on that," Jen retorted, not altogether jokingly. "But, if you must." She heaved a sigh. "What do you want me to do?"

"Can you keep the boys out of the house for a while? Say, a half hour or so?"

Jen gave her a dry look. "Do you think the mention of the words 'pizza in town' would work?"

Elizabeth came up with a genuine smile. "I have a hunch it might."

"Then I'm outta here." Jen started for the kitchen door, but hesitated with her hand on the screen doorknob. "You're sure you'll be okay?"

Elizabeth shrugged. "As you said a couple of weeks ago, what can he do to me?"

"Well, all things considered," Jen said grimly, pulling the door open. "In regards to Lyon, only God, or the Devil, would know."

No, Elizabeth thought, feeling deserted and scared as she watched Jen lope around the side of the house. She knew, or at least, she had a stomach-gripping suspicion of what Lyon could do.

Her options were reduced to one, and Elizabeth knew it. Lyon had won. He hadn't been bragging or bluffing before. He *was* holding all the trump cards. And now she had little choice but to deal with him.

Elizabeth drew her bleak gaze from the screen door and took a step toward the dining-room archway. What had he told her earlier? she mused, eyes narrowing, lips growing tight. Something to the effect of there being no law that states that he must tell everything he knows? Well, there was no law that she knew of stating that she had to play the game by his rules.

Lyon had won. But by damn, Elizabeth vowed, her anger returning as she crossed the dining room, she would do what she must, use whatever trick came to hand to insure his victory wasn't all that sweet and satisfying.

He had won. Lyon knew it the moment Elizabeth walked into the room. For all her attitude of bravado, defeat was stamped into her features, her posture, her eyes.

Elation soared through Lyon, quickly followed by an odd sensation of regret.

Elizabeth had looked so beautiful, so excitingly magnificent with her hair swirling around her shoulders and her eyes blazing defiance when she had confronted him less than an hour ago.

That was the woman Lyon wanted, that tigress ready to defend her young with tooth and claw. Desire, hot and strong, had surged through him at the sight of her. It had taken every ounce of control Lyon possessed to keep from tossing Elizabeth to the floor of Jen's living room in broad daylight and tangling with her there on the rough fibers of the braided rug.

He had wanted to feel her claws, her teeth sinking into his flesh, raking his skin. He had been on fire to sink his own teeth, his fingers, his body into hers, feel her anger at him turn to a fury of passion for him.

God! What madness, Lyon reflected, watching her move toward him. What exciting, delicious madness.

Controlling the crazy impulse to pounce on her before had been difficult. Now, as Elizabeth stormed to within a foot of him, her eyes narrowed, her stance militant, Lyon experienced a sexual thrill so intense, he knew, instinctively, that keeping his hands off her wasn't going to get easier anytime soon. It was fortunate for Elizabeth that Mitch, Jen and her boys were around somewhere. Very fortunate.

"All right. All right, you creep," she literally spat the words at him. "State your terms."

Yes, yes, this was the Elizabeth he wanted, Lyon rejoiced in silent approval. Not a defeated supplicant, or even the sweet young girl of ten years ago, but this glorious creature, standing tall and straight, eyes ablaze with challenge.

"Creep?" Lyon repeated in a cool drawl, somehow managing to conceal the anticipation singing through his veins. "Is that any way to address your son's father?"

"Trash it, Cantrell," Elizabeth snarled. "What are the terms of the blackmail you have the gall to refer to as a bargain?"

"As stated," he returned, unperturbed by her tone and aggression. "Bring Mitch and come live with me."

"In what capacity?" Elizabeth shot back. "As your exclusive, live-in whore?"

Lyon went stiff. He felt his facial muscles lock, his hands clench into fists. "No," he said in harsh denial, even as he admitted the kernel of truth in her charge. "As the mother of *our* son."

The faint smile that flickered over Elizabeth's lips called him a liar in silent eloquence. "For how long... a few weeks, a few months?"

Lyon felt his stomach muscles tighten. How long? He ran a slow, encompassing gaze over her face, her form. Even with the gripping muscles, he had the sensation of the bottom dropping out of his stomach. How long? How many years did he have left?

"I haven't decided as yet," he said, more than a little surprised at the steadiness of his voice. "I'll wait and see how things go."

"Things?" Elizabeth actually sneered the word.

"Yes... things," he repeated, treating her to another searing, overall look.

She was visibly getting angrier by the minute.

He was getting hotter; he prayed not visibly.

"And do you have a time schedule to begin your game of playing house."

"Today."

"Today!" Elizabeth yelped. "You are out of your skull. I was packing to leave when you arrived here."

Lyon's shrug indicated an indifference he was far from feeling. "In that case, you can transfer your things from here to my place."

Elizabeth made a noise gritting her teeth. "I can't do that. I have an apartment full of furniture, a job. I'm scheduled for a flight out of Philly International the day after tomorrow."

"I'll take care of all that," Lyon said, flipping one hand, as if made bored by mere details.

"Take care of it?" Elizabeth stared at him in amazement. "If you think I'd allow your flunkies to paw through my things, you are out of your mind!"

"You're getting repetitious," he bit out, growing impatient, and unsure whether with her or himself. "But, to put your mind at rest, I'd have professional movers clean out your apartment, not my flunkies." His mouth curved wryly around the last word. "As to your job—" he shrugged again "—I will personally arrange a leave of absence for you."

"No, you will not!" Elizabeth said emphatically. "I will not give up my career to become your full-time anything. I will make my own arrangements."

"All right." Lyon watched as her eyes flickered with unexpected surprise, then he hit her with his condition. "But you will leave Mitch here, with me."

"Leave Mitch?" Elizabeth's voice was faint, her eyes wide, her face pale, deathly pale.

Lyon's stomach gave a painful lurch, proving the bottom had not fallen out. He felt sick with disgust, self-disgust. Telling himself that she had earned any form of retribution he dished out didn't help much; he still felt sick. The sensation backed him up.

"All right, damn you, take him with you," he said, turning away from her, because it was either retreat or gather her into his arms. "I'll give you two weeks," he called, not looking back as he strode for the front door. "And if you're not back by then, I'll come after you." Pausing in the open doorway, he swung to give her a drilling stare. "Another thing," he said, his voice harsh with warning.

"Wh-what?" Elizabeth nervously wet her lips.

Lyon swallowed a groan, and growled, "When you return, Mitch better damn well know that I'm his father." Striding across the threshold, he resisted an impulse to slam the door, shutting it quietly instead.

* * *

The scheduled flight to Phoenix was uneventful, smooth as silk out and back, allowing Elizabeth time to think, too much time to think.

She had yet to broach the subject of his parentage with Mitch. Not that she had lacked opportunity. Elizabeth had had ample time for an in-depth discussion with her son throughout the long drive back to their apartment. She simply hadn't known where to begin.

And it wasn't even as if Mitch didn't know that his father was alive; he did. Going against her parents' advice that she take the easy way by telling Mitch at the outset that his father was dead, Elizabeth had opted for an explanation as close to the truth as possible.

In simple terms that Mitch could comprehend, Elizabeth had told him that the relationship between her and his father had disintegrated, and that they had separated before either one of them realized she was going to have a child. She had made a point to add that she was positive, had he known, Mitch's father would have loved him every bit as much as she did herself.

In his innocence, Mitch had not only accepted her explanation, but believed every word.

So, now, how did she begin to explain that Mr. Cantrell—the very same Mr. Cantrell she had chas-

tised Mitch for about talking to strangers—was in fact
no stranger at all, but Mitch's natural father? Elizabeth had scourged her mind for an answer, a way to
explain. Since her mind had appeared closed to the
subject, she had not as yet talked to him. She had,
however, talked to her other family members . . . and
talked, and talked.

Jen had objected loud and angrily to Elizabeth's
decision to comply with the terms of Lyon's bargain.
Throughout most of the last night of Elizabeth's visit
to her brother's house, and all the way to the car as she
loaded the trunk with their suitcases, Jen had argued,
pleaded, cajoled Elizabeth to reconsider the enormity
of the step she was about to take, to trust in her lawyer to find a way to resolve the problem. Elizabeth had
been steadfast in her response.

"I can't take that chance."

Although, while explaining the situation to her
parents, Elizabeth had smoothed the edges of the
particulars of Lyon's demand, they, too, raised strong
objections to her plans, advising her in effect to wait
and see what developed at the hearing.

Elizabeth's answer to her parents had echoed the
one she had given to Jen.

Her brother, Chuck, on the other hand, merely exploded, long distance, ranting and raving, and threatening bodily harm to Lyon in the near future.

While trying to soothe Chuck's flaming temper, Elizabeth had told him basically the same as she had told his wife and their parents, adding her assurance that she and Mitch would be all right.

It was all more than a little dispiriting, depressing, wearying.

The only advance Elizabeth had made to comply with Lyon's dictate—and she couldn't think of it as anything other than a dictate—concerned her work. Citing the need for some time to correct some personal domestic problems, she had asked for and been granted a thirty-day leave of absence, beginning with the completion of this round-trip Phoenix swing.

According to the flight engineer, they would be arriving at Philadelphia on schedule. Then Elizabeth would be free, at least so far as her job went, for a month.

The task awaiting her was daunting. Elizabeth had to arrange for movers to transport her belongings from her apartment on the outskirts of Philly, to the pile of stone of Lyon's, all the way up near where the three state lines of Pennsylvania, New York and New Jersey converged. She also had to arrange for the transferal of Mitch's school records...and she didn't as yet know where he would be attending school. She hoped Lyon would agree to enrolling Mitch in the same public school she herself had attended, but knowing Lyon, she—

"Wake up, Elizabeth."

The captain's stern voice intruded into the morass of Elizabeth's introspection. Suddenly alert, she jerked upright, and slanted a wary look at the tight features of the man seated next to her at the controls.

Captain Bland... wasn't.

Of all times and flights, Elizabeth thought, repressing a sigh, why had this happened to her now, with this particular flight, with this particular captain? Captain Bland, a twenty-odd-year veteran with the airline, was famous—or infamous—for his disapproval of females in the cockpit. He was a known chauvinist, with a capital *C*.

"You did hear the message about the wind shear at Philly, didn't you?"

Oh, hell. Elizabeth clamped her lips against the words, gathered her courage, and confessed.

"No, sir."

"I thought not." Captain Bland was not pleased. "It's coming through again, would you care to listen in?"

Elizabeth did. The wind shear factor was not as strong as some she had heard about and even experienced at other airports, but any wind shear was dangerous.

Elizabeth felt no sense of urgency or real concern. Though gruff and stringent he might be, Captain

Bland had the reputation of being one of the best pilots, of any airline.

"Do you want to take it in?"

Elizabeth turned in her seat to stare in utter amazement at her captain. Neither his expression nor his tone had lost its sternness, but there was a challenging gleam, an actual twinkle in the depths of his cool gray eyes, which she couldn't resist.

"Yes," she answered at once with unabashed enthusiasm. "Yes, sir!"

"The controls are yours." So saying, he relinquished the guidance of the big jet plane into her slender hands.

A deep and centered sense of calm settled over Elizabeth as she took over the controls. Every other concern fled from her mind: Lyon, the tasks waiting for her attention at home, even thoughts of Mitch.

Second only to Mitch and her family, flying was the joy of Elizabeth's life. With cool, precise professionalism, she eased the jet down, down, through the wind shear and onto the runway.

"Awright, Liz!" the captain cried as the wheels made contact with the tarmac with just the slightest bump. "Good girl."

Blinking in shocked surprise, Elizabeth spared a glance at him, and blinked again when she found him grinning at her, one hand raised, thumb up. On the spot, she vowed that never again would she make the mistake of thinking of Captain Bland with a capital *C*.

When she left the airport a short while later there was a jaunty spring in her steps, a spring that had been missing ever since her return from the mountains.

Though sweet, Elizabeth's sense of euphoria was short-lived. It lasted up until the moment she collected Mitch from the neighbor who took care of him during her absences while flying.

She had to talk to Mitch, explain, but where to begin? The question plagued Elizabeth all through the preparation and consuming of dinner.

"Er... honey, I'd like to talk to you about your father," she began while they worked together clearing the dishes from the table and loading the dishwasher.

"What about him?" Mitch asked—with a notable lack of interest.

"Well..." Elizabeth cleared her throat. "You see... that is..."

Mitch stopped what he was doing to give her a purely pre-teen look that said, "What's your problem?"

Elizabeth stared at her darling monster of a son in despair for a moment, then she drew a deep breath and blurted out, "You remember Mr. Cantrell?"

"Geez, Mom, I'm not a baby, you know," Mitch groused. "'Course I remember him. He's a pretty neat guy." His boy-handsome face twisted into a man's frown. "What's he got to do with anything?"

Oh, brother, Elizabeth groaned in silent misery. What indeed! How to do it? Where to begin? She was asking herself, raking her mushy gray matter for inspiration, when Mitch leaned forward to peer into her eyes.

"Are you in there, lady?" he inquired in what had become an ongoing joke between them.

Elizabeth laughed, immediately flung back to the beginning of their private joke. Mitch was five at the time. It was Christmas. She had been asleep, as all decent folks were at four-thirty in the morning. Mitch had crawled into bed with her, pried up one of her eyelids, and in a coaxing voice, asked, "Are you in there, lady?"

"Yes, love, I'm in here," Elizabeth answered him now, as she had answered him then.

"Mom?"

Elizabeth heard and understood the confusion in his voice. Mitch was wondering why she hadn't reacted now as she had that Christmas morning, and each time since then, with an attack of her tickling fingers.

Her laughter died on a sigh of regret. She had to tell him. Now. Get it over with, she prodded herself, girding for the worse, hoping for the best.

"Mr. Cantrell is your real father, Mitch." There, it was said. Elizabeth caught her bottom lip between her teeth, and waited for his reaction.

"Mr. Cantrell?" Mitch gave her a funny look, not unlike the one he'd bestowed on her when he discovered there was no real Santa Claus. "Are you sure?"

This time her bout of laughter had too much the sound of incipient hysteria. "Ah...yes, Mitch, I'm positive," she said, smothering the urge to follow her laughter with a wailing sob.

"Mr. Cantrell, huh?" Mitch's expression turned adult-pensive as he mulled over the information.

Elizabeth waited, and waited, holding her breath, fearful for herself, hurting for him, actually afraid of what he would say.

"Mr. Cantrell. Yeah. Okay, I guess. Pretty decent."

His calm acceptance literally blew Elizabeth's mind. She had expected...what? Angry shouts? Tears? Accusations? Yes, all of those and more. "Pretty decent"? Would she, or for that matter, any parent, ever understand the resilience of the young?

"Is that all you have to say?" she asked in a soft, stunned voice.

"Well...no." Mitch shifted his feet and glanced down, as if fascinated by the pattern in the floor tiles.

"I'll answer any questions as honestly as I can, honey," she offered, giving in to an impulse to smooth his shorn, tawny bristles.

"Er," Mitch glanced up at her, then quickly looked down again. "Does he...I mean, do you know if...like...well...does he like me?"

Elizabeth felt a sharp pang in her heart and a hot sting in her eyes. Reaching out, she drew him into her arms. "Yes, Mitch, he does," she said around the hard lump in her throat. "Mr. Cantrell likes you very much."

"That's good, I guess." Mitch lifted his head from her chest to sneak a look at her face. "Isn't it? I mean, it's okay with you that he likes me?"

Elizabeth felt the tremor in his slim body all the way to her soul. "Yes, love, it's okay with me." She heard, felt, his sigh of relief, and wished with everything inside of her that she didn't have to go on. But she did, and she knew it. "In fact, honey," she said, starting slowly then rushing to finish. "Mr. Cantrell—your father—likes you so much, he wants us to come live with him."

Stillness. Absolute stillness. Elizabeth could barely hear or feel Mitch breathing. Come to that, she was barely breathing herself.

"Live with him?" he finally murmured. "You mean like a family?"

"Yes," she answered, praying, for his sake if not her own, that it was the truth.

"I'd have a father, a real dad?" The quivery, hopeful sound of his voice tore at her heart.

"Yes, Mitch, you'd have a real dad," she promised, certain in her own mind that that, if nothing else, was the truth. Lyon had evinced genuine concern for his son; he'd be a real dad.

"We'd live up there, in the mountains?" Disentangling himself from her protective embrace, Mitch shuffled backward to look at her with open curiosity. "All the time, winter and summer?"

"Yes, all the time, winter and summer," she said, while amending silently, *at least you would.*

"Do you want to?" he asked, again in the hopeful tone that left her with one answer only.

"If you do, yes." Elizabeth didn't see the need to add that his father had given her no choice.

Mitch was quiet a minute, a long minute. Elizabeth would have sworn she could see the wheels turning inside his perfectly shaped head. Then he grinned, nearly destroying her by looking exactly like his father.

"Okay, then, yes!" he shouted, beginning to fidget with excitement and anticipation. "Let's go!"

Seven

Incredible.

Elizabeth peered through the gathering darkness as another low rumble of thunder rolled around the edges of the mountain.

"Gonna storm pretty soon." The weather forecast came from Mitch, seated on the seat next to her, smothering a yawn and making a valiant effort to stay awake.

"Um," Elizabeth murmured in agreement. "I just hope we beat the downpour to the house."

Mitch mumbled in response.

"What?" Elizabeth frowned and slid a quick glance at her son. A smile softened her tension-tightened mouth; Mitch had lost the battle to sleep.

Another low boom reverberated through the thickening atmosphere, still some distance away, but growing steadily nearer.

More than incredible, it was kind of weird, Elizabeth thought, reflecting on the growling approach of a storm on the very first night of her arrival in her hometown six weeks ago.

The black-topped road snaked up through the mountain, shrouded by lowering clouds misting the trees with wispy gray tendrils.

Tension pulling at the muscles at the back of her neck and across her shoulders, Elizabeth squinted through the windshield. It was nearly dark now, and it was still only late afternoon, late afternoon of the last day remaining of the two weeks Lyon had allotted to her.

He was probably prowling and growling louder than the storm moving in, Elizabeth mused, shrugging her shoulders to loosen the tension and chase the sudden chill of trepidation skipping down her spine. And his visage was more than likely darker than the thunderheads.

The moving van should have arrived at Lyon's house two days ago and, since she had pulled out in her car right behind the van, she should have pulled into Lyon's driveway right behind the van.

Elizabeth felt certain that Lyon had spent the ensuing two days striding back and forth between the heavy oak door and the long windows at the front of the house, cursing her for dawdling along the way.

And dawdle along the way was indeed exactly what Elizabeth had done, with cool deliberation. Lyon had given her two weeks. Elizabeth had determined to take every day of those two weeks. It was a small form of rebellion, perhaps, but satisfying nonetheless.

Lightning streaked overhead, casting the wind-tossed trees in an eerie white glow. Elizabeth winced, and tightened her grip on the steering wheel.

Would she never get to the top of this dratted road? The self question brought a wry smile to her lips. The day before yesterday, yesterday, that very morning, Elizabeth had felt not the slightest compunction about not hastening toward her journey's end. Quite the opposite; she had derived grim pleasure from dragging out to the last moment her arrival at Lyon's mountain retreat.

Elizabeth had known, of course, before she had locked the door of her apartment for the very last time, that she would not be taking a direct route, meekly following in the wake of the moving van.

The idea had come to her earlier that week, a product of a radio advertisement. The announcer had caught her attention with the enthusiasm in his voice as he extolled the delights in store for the entire family with a visit to an amusement park near Shamokin, which, frankly, Elizabeth had never heard of before.

The location of the park was out of her way, calling for a detour of her route. But then . . .

Elizabeth chuckled, recalling the look on Mitch's face when, at an intersection, the cumbersome moving van had continued on, while she had made a right turn onto a different highway.

"Hey, Mom!" he'd cried, looking back over his bony shoulder. "You're going the wrong way."

"No, I'm not," she had answered in a light, burden-freed tone. "We're making a side trip."

"Where to?" he'd demanded.

"You'll see," she had caroled. "Trust me, kid, you're gonna love it."

And Mitch had loved it, every second of the dizzying rides, every minute of the soaking pool and water slides, and every momentary stop to renew his energy at every other food stand they passed.

Elizabeth had registered at a nearby motel for one night; they had stayed for two. The warm, crystal-clear late summer weather had been an allure neither she nor Mitch could resist.

Incredible.

Elizabeth grimaced as another bolt of lightning seared the sky, followed by a louder roar of thunder.

The balmy weather had held until just before she had begun the drive up the road to Lyon's house.

It was enough to give her the creeps. It did give her the shivers. Was she, Elizabeth asked in silent despair, forever fated to exit or enter Lyon's house through a sheeting downpour?

Apparently so, for large drops of rain began pelting the windshield as she pulled the car into the curving drive leading to Lyon's den.

Where in hell was she?

The question had been resounding inside Lyon's head ever since the moving van had arrived, with no sign of Elizabeth trailing behind it.

He had given her two weeks. It was now late in the afternoon of the last day of those two weeks. Lyon was beginning to roar... if in frustrated silence.

Reflecting the worsening weather conditions, he stormed through the house, always returning to the front windows and door, scanning the driveway for a sign of Elizabeth's car.

Nothing.

Damn her. Where could she be? Lyon railed, a worried frown drawing his gold-tipped brows together at the evidence of the lowering sky.

All hell was going to break loose, and soon, outside with the storm, and inside, within him.

Had Elizabeth run from him again?

There it was, the root cause of the confusion of emotions churning to the boiling point inside Lyon. Dammit! If she had run away, he'd . . .

What?

Lyon turned away from the window, but he couldn't turn aside from the question. What would he do if Elizabeth had taken it into her defiant mind to send her belongings to him, while running away with the possessions most valuable to Lyon—herself and their son?

Raking his hand through tawny hair already ruffled by repeated rakings, Lyon strode to the door. Pulling it open, he stood on the threshold, willing his eyes to see around the curve in the driveway, and further down the winding road beyond.

A white bright streak of lightning flashed, tearing jagged rips in the mass of angry-looking black clouds overhead.

The storm was going to be a bitch. Lyon knew it, and with the knowing, knew fear, as well.

Elizabeth.

A real sense of uneasiness invaded Lyon's stomach. She had to come, show up soon, because, if she didn't, he was afraid he'd go slowly out of his mind until he could track her down, find her.

It was almost funny, he thought, watching the trees bend before the wind, hearing the soughing rustle of the branches and leaves. Almost.

He had spent the majority of the last two weeks moving to the phone, backing off, then moving to it again, torn between the need to check up on her and an inner cautioning voice telling him to refrain from applying additional pressure to her.

Lyon wanted her here, now, with their son beside her, ready if not willing to abide by his wishes.

Arrogant bastard.

A crooked smile touched Lyon's lips. His wishes. Ha! Try demands. Who the hell was he, anyway, to issue orders to Elizabeth?

He was the injured party in this instance. Hadn't she robbed him of the formative years of his son's life? Hadn't she stolen from him the joy of watching, sharing each new moment of Mitch's growth; his first smile, his first words; his first steps; his first day at school?

Yes, Lyon reminded his weakening self. Elizabeth had stolen all those moments and more from him. Hell, Lyon thought, glaring at the driveway as he felt a sharp pang in his chest. Even now he had no way of knowing if he would ever hear his son call him Dad.

Where was she? Lyon questioned, raising his eyes from the drive to the fast-moving storm above. It was going to rip loose any minute and—

A fat drop of rain struck Lyon's forehead, bringing his thoughts up sharp. Lowering his gaze, he stared at the rapidly accumulating quarter-size wet marks

staining the stone entrance steps. Becoming riddled
with an unfamiliar sense of anxiety, Lyon lifted his
eyes, and felt a never-before experienced surge of relief. A car was pulling into the long driveway...Elizabeth's car.

Spinning around, Lyon strode into the cavernous
hall and to a deep closet to the right. Yanking the door
open, he withdrew a large striped umbrella from the
scabbard attached to the side of his golf bag. He unfurled the umbrella as he exited the house, and hit the
button, opening it, as he descended the stone steps,
just as Elizabeth brought the car to a stop.

Was he in a rage? Elizabeth studied Lyon's expression as he strode toward the car. She couldn't tell; his
features were set, unrevealing. She sighed. Well, angry or not, at least he had come to meet them with
protective covering. Keeping her gaze fixed on Lyon,
she reached across the seat to nudge her son's shoulder.

"Wake up, Mitch," she called. "We're ho—here."

"Huh?" Mitch mumbled, shifting on the seat.
"What did you say, Mom?"

"I said we are..." Elizabeth's voice was drowned
by an earth-shaking boom of thunder, followed by a
yelped exclamation from beside her.

"Holy moly!"

At the same instant, the car door was flung open. "Let's go," Lyon shouted over the continuing thunder and wailing wind. "One at a time. You first, Elizabeth. Mitch, crawl over the console and be ready to run for it when I come back for you."

He didn't wait for a response, from either mother or son. Elizabeth was hustled from the car and literally run into the house, to immediately be left alone, standing inside the door, as Lyon made a return dash outside to collect Mitch.

"Boy!" Mitch exclaimed, running into the house. "That's some storm out there."

"Decent, huh?" Elizabeth said, feeling strained, but trying for some semblance of normalcy.

"More like awesome," Mitch answered, sharing his infectious grin with both her and Lyon.

"Awesome, isn't it," Lyon drawled, grinning back at Mitch, while sliding an amused look at Elizabeth. "And what do you think of the house?" he asked, indicating the place with a flick of his wrist.

Mitch followed Lyon's gesture with eyes growing bigger and brighter by the second. "Geez, it's jumbo, ain't it?" he murmured in a hushed, impressed tone. "I mean, like, major awesome."

"Yes." Lyon laughed. "And this is merely the front foyer. My father—" he hesitated for the length of a heartbeat "—your grandfather thought in major awesome terms," he continued wryly. "Wait until you see the rest of the house."

"When can I?" Mitch responded eagerly. Then, "Oh, wow!" he breathed, skimming a wide-eyed stare up the broad, curved staircase. He moved toward it, as if drawn by invisible cords.

"Mitchell," Elizabeth said in a tone of warning caution. "Wait until you've been—"

"Is there anything I can do to help, Lyon?"

Elizabeth started and turned at the sound of the soft and pleasant, slightly familiar voice. He was extremely good-looking, around Lyon's age, and there was something... A frown shadowed her brow. She felt she knew him, or should know him, but from where and when?

"Ah, there you are," Lyon greeted the man with a smile. "Come meet my... guests." When the man came to a stop before them, Lyon went on, "Elizabeth, perhaps you remember Hunt Canon, he and your brother were good friends at one time."

"Yes, of course," Elizabeth said, smiling in sudden recognition. "How are you, Hunt?"

"Hanging in there," he replied, strolling closer to her. "And I don't have to ask how you are," he went on in a wry tone seemingly aimed more at himself than at her. "I can see for myself that you are more beautiful than any woman should be allowed to be." He arched a brow at Lyon. "Isn't that right?"

"Close enough," Lyon drawled, sharing what was obviously a private joke between them, while managing to thoroughly confuse Elizabeth at the same time. He shifted his gaze to the boy now standing at the base of the staircase. "And this is . . ."

"Your son," Hunt finished, his oddly cynical expression softening with compassion.

"Yes, my son, Mitchell," Lyon echoed in a strong voice. "But I'm sure he won't object if you call him Mitch, will you . . . son?"

Mitch looked startled for a moment, then a broad smile lighted his face. "No . . . Dad."

Elizabeth swallowed, but couldn't seem to dislodge the lump in her throat—which felt about the size of the mountain they were perched atop.

"Are you still living in the area, Hunt?" she asked, clearing her throat, and desperate to change the subject of fathers and sons.

"You might say that," he answered, cracking a smile that was breathtaking in its sudden and unexpected brilliance and charm. Stepping closer to her, he extended his hand. "I'm working for Lyon now, and I hope you'll be—" he sliced a dry look at Lyon before continuing "—comfortable here." The eyes he returned to her were filled with understanding. "If there is anything you need, don't hesitate to call on me."

In a strange way, Elizabeth felt comforted just staring into the man's compassionate eyes. "Thank you, Hunt," she murmured, sliding her hand into his. "I . . . I appreciate the offer."

He bestowed a gentle smile on her, then turned to grin at her son, offering his hand to him, as well. "Mitch, I have a feeling that you and I are going to be great friends. What do you think?"

Always friendly, always outgoing and, at least for the most part for Elizabeth, always exhaustingly "up," Mitch laughed and slapped his palm against Hunt's. "I think I need something to eat."

"Mitchell!" Elizabeth exclaimed in chastisement, stepping into her role of always being, or trying to be, the perfect mother. "Don't be fresh."

"He's not being fresh at all," Lyon put in around a chuckle, appearing all at once relaxed and at ease. "He's home. He's hungry and . . ."

"And I have a huge home-made pizza in the kitchen," Hunt inserted, again finishing for his employer.

"You made it?" Mitch's eyes grew round with instant respect; any man who could make pizza was top dog in his book. "All by yourself?"

Hunt's lips twitched, as if he were putting up a valiant fight against a roar of laughter. "All by myself," he intoned solemnly. "You learn these things when you've got a demanding younger sibling to contend with. I'll teach you how to make it, too, if you like."

"I like!" Mitch whooped, swinging away from the stairs. "Let's go!"

"You must clean up first, young man," Elizabeth ordered, sending a stern if somewhat helpless look between the two men, both of whom were grinning at the boy and wearing like, adoring expressions.

The weary note underlying her adamant tone of voice set the men into action.

Taking her arm, Lyon started for Mitch, and the stairs. "I'll show you to your rooms," he said, slinging one arm around Mitch's shoulders as he stepped up beside him. "Wait until you see yours, Mitch." Urging mother and son along, he started up the stairs.

Elizabeth took the first step, then stopped cold. "Our case," she said. "I have a suitcase in the car."

"I'll collect it," Hunt offered, heading for the door. He glanced over his shoulder to smile at Mitch. "Then I'll come and collect you and introduce you to a fully loaded pizza. Okay?"

"Okay!" Mitch cried, fairly dancing up the stairs between Elizabeth and Lyon.

When they attained the broad landing at the top of the staircase, Lyon steered them along a wide hallway, then turned left at an intersecting corridor. "Your room's this way, Mitch."

"Geez, a guy could get lost up here," Mitch said, glancing around with avid interest.

"You'll soon get familiar with it," Lyon said, coming to a halt before a door midway along the corridor. He grasped the doorknob, then shot a grin at Mitch. "Besides, there will probably be days when you might want to get lost." He lowered his voice to a stage whisper. "You know, like from your mother, when she's put out with you?"

"Hey, yeah," Mitch whispered back, conspiratorially, sliding a sly look at Elizabeth. "You mean, like when she's after me about homework and stuff?"

"Yeah," Lyon agreed, nodding.

Elizabeth felt torn between laughter and despair. She was genuinely happy for her son, who, from all appearances, had found the father he so desperately wanted. But, for herself, well . . .

"Elizabeth?" Lyon prodded her from the quandary. "Don't you want to see the room?"

She blinked, only then realizing that he had swung the door open. Mitch was standing in the doorway, his face a study of wonder and delight. Moving to stand behind him, Elizabeth examined the interior.

The room was the answer to every boy's dream of a personal and private sanctum sanctorum. It was decorated in shades of browns and greens, not unlike the traditional colors of camouflage, with here and there splashes of the new colors of white and sand.

Everything was neat and in place, and with just a cursory inspection, Elizabeth discovered new meaning in the word "everything."

All of Mitch's belongings were there, along with a seemingly truckload of new things, from toys to sports equipment to an up-to-the-minute, state-of-the-art personal computer, holding pride of place on top of a curved computer desk.

The sight was enough to make a young boy dance with ecstatic glee... which Mitch did, in ever-widening circles around the room. He was bouncing back and forth, ricocheting from one new acquisition to another, when Hunt entered the room.

"What say, sport," he called, surrendering the suitcase in his hand to Lyon. "Like your room?"

"It's decent!" Mitch cried, running to Hunt to grab hold of his hand. "Come look at all this neat stuff!"

"I want to see it, all of it," Hunt said, laughing. "But first, I don't know about you, kid, but I'm hungry. What do you say, ready for some pizza?"

Mitch made a sharp about-face and shot for the door. "Awright! Let's go!"

"Mitchell, wash your hands," Elizabeth said, leveling her sternest parental look on him.

"Aw, geez," he grumbled, while stomping into his very own bathroom to obey. He bolted back into the room less than thirty seconds later, his hands dotted with drops of water. "Okay, they're washed," he said, holding them in the air for inspection as he made another dash for the door. "Comin', Mom?"

"I want to show your mother to her room, son," Lyon answered for her, while smiling at Mitch. "We'll be down in a little while."

"Take your time," Hunt drawled, strolling from the room after Mitch. "It's a very large pizza."

There was a heartbeat and a half of silence, uncomfortable silence, then Lyon gave a sweeping gesture of his free hand to the open doorway. "After you," he said in a suspiciously pleasant tone.

Eyeing him warily, Elizabeth walked by him, only to stand, nervous and irresolute in the corridor.

"Back the way we came," he directed her. "First door to the right at the head of the stairs."

Elizabeth retraced their path along the corridor, then came to a stop, staring at the solid wood door, arms hanging limply by her sides.

Reaching around her, Lyon released the fancy brass latch and pushed the door open. "It's safe," he said in a bone-dry voice. "Not booby-trapped or anything."

Elizabeth was beyond appreciation of the humor in the situation, intended or otherwise. Stiff, unsmiling, she took two steps into the room, suppressed a gasp of shock, and stopped dead.

The room was beautiful, easily the most beautiful
bedroom she had ever seen. The colors were muted,
raspberry, mauve, swirls of rich cream. The furniture
had an old, heavy but elegant look, lavish with polish
and tender loving care. Her personal things, hair-
brush, hand mirror, small jewelry case, were placed on
top of one dresser. Elizabeth knew instinctively that
her foldables were neatly tucked away inside the deep
dresser drawers, and that the rest of her clothes were
hanging in a closet.

But it was not her room; it was *his* room.

She had been under no illusions from the outset.
Elizabeth had known exactly what would be expected
of her from the instant Lyon had issued his proposition. He hadn't had to elaborate on his dictum, or to
rephrase his invitation of "Bring Mitch and come live
with me" to "Bring Mitch and come sleep with me."

She had spent two weeks of restless days and sleep-
less nights tormented by wildly arousing, crushingly
humiliating memories of her willing, eager participa-
tion in the drama she and Lyon had played out on the
floor in front of the fireplace in his library.

Yes, Elizabeth had known what to expect; she had
even accepted her fate. Or, she had thought she had.
But now, faced with the prospective scene of her de-
basement, she dug her heels in, literally and figura-
tively.

"I will not sleep with you, Lyon." Her voice was tight, uneven in tenor, but rock-solid in conviction.

"You agreed." His voice was soft, but as solid.

Elizabeth fought against a shiver of awareness. He was standing behind her, close behind her. His warm breath caressed the back of her head. His scent teased her senses. The heat from his body, his very nearness, sent a shock wave of weakness through her. Elizabeth forced her breath from her body in an even tempo.

"I agreed to come live with you, to stay with Mitch," she said, holding her fingers stiff and straight to keep them from curling in, to dig nervously into her palms. "I did not agree to sleep with you."

"Elizabeth, be realistic," he began.

"No!" she shouted, whirling to confront him. "No, I will not listen to any more of your threats." She had reached the end of her tether after weeks of accumulated tension. Her control, and her breathing tempo, flew out the proverbial window. "I'm here, and I'll stay here, for however long you decide I must." Her breathing was now ragged, her voice harsh with strain.

"Damn, Elizabeth, you're crying!"

"I'm not," she cried the denial on a broken sob.

The suitcase fell from his hand to land on the plush carpet with a soft, unnoticed thud. "Calm down," Lyon said in an imploring tone that escaped her. "You're trembling, and you're becoming hysterical," he went on, raising his hands to grasp her shoulders.

"No, don't," Elizabeth shook her head and shrank back, shrugging off his hands. "Don't touch me." Lifting one hand to her face, she wiped at the tears streaming down her cheeks. "To keep Mitch, I'll stay here, I'll even play the role of friend and companion to you, if that's what you want, but I will not play the who—"

"Don't say that word again," Lyon snapped, jamming his hands into his pockets, as if to keep from doing something foolish, or violent.

"I won't give up my job, my career, either," she gasped between deep, gulping breaths.

"I haven't asked you to give up—"

"I'm not finished," she shouted, past the point of listening, hearing. "Because you've given me no choice, I'll stay. But I won't cater to your every whim. And I absolutely will not sleep with you." Drawing herself up proudly, she flung down her own ultimatum. "You can take it or leave it. Or you can go to hell."

"I'll take it."

Lyon's quietly voiced acceptance took the wind from her sails. Her chest heaving, her vision blurry, Elizabeth peered at him in stunned silence. What game was he playing now? she wondered, brushing the tears from her face with trembling fingertips.

"I said, I'll take it," Lyon repeated.

"I . . . heard you."

"But you don't believe me," he accurately guessed her thoughts. "Or trust me. Do you?"

"No," she confessed in a quavery whisper.

"No, of course not." He exhaled a long, shuddering sigh, as if he had been the one doing all the shouting, having emotional fits. "I suppose I can't blame you for that." He grimaced. "I haven't given you a helluva lot of reason to trust me, have I?"

"No," Elizabeth said, underscoring her mistrust by watching him warily. "Your methods produced the opposite, in fact."

"Right." Lyon dug his fingers through his hair, drawing her reluctant attention to not only the wild disorder of the tawny mane, but to the shaggy length of it, as well. "Look, we're going to have to talk about this, set the parameters of our relationship, but—"

"There is no relationship between us!" Elizabeth broke in, cutting him off.

"Come on, Elizabeth, think," Lyon retorted. "We are going to be sharing this house. More importantly, we are going to be sharing our son." He paused to draw a harsh breath, and lower his voice. "Under those conditions, you must understand that there has got to be a working relationship between us because, unless we come to an agreement, we will tear Mitch apart."

Elizabeth didn't want to understand, see his point of view. She wanted to rant and rave, scream accusations at him. Trust? Hah! She longed to fling the cold, ruthless manner of his demeaning, soul-destroying payoff and desertion of her and their unborn child back into his face, with all the force of an accumulation of ten years' worth of bitterness.

She wanted to, and even drew a deep breath, steadying herself for her spate of condemnation, but all that issued through her trembling lips was a sigh. What was the use, now, after all this time? Pouring her sense of outrage over him at this late stage wouldn't prove a thing, or alter their existing circumstances.

Her long sigh ended in surrender, not in defeat, but acknowledgment of her primary consideration. Her feelings were valid, and important, but... though she was justifiably furious and adamant in her determination to defy him, she was equally cognizant of the emotional damage she—they—could inflict on their son, the innocent bystander to their power struggle.

Elizabeth couldn't do it, she simply could not be the one to wipe the glow of newfound joy from her son's bright young face and shining eyes.

"Elizabeth?" Lyon's tone held a prodding edge of growing impatience. "*Do* you understand?"

Elizabeth's spirits slumped; but her spine stayed straight, her shoulders squared. "Yes," she confessed. "I do understand."

The breath Lyon expelled had the sound of being long pent up inside his chest. "Okay," he said, sud-

denly brisk, all business. "First things first. Let's get
settled, then present a united front for Mitch." He
slanted a cautious look at her. "All right?"

"All right," she agreed, suppressing yet another
sigh. "Where do I go to get settled?"

Scooping the suitcase from the floor, Lyon pivoted
and strode back into the corridor. "You can take your
pick," he invited with a sweeping hand motion.
"There are sixteen bedrooms in this barn."

"Sixteen!" Elizabeth exclaimed, gaping at him. "I
hope you have more than Hunt for help here."

Lyon gave her a "get serious" look. "Of course I
have," he merely said. "There are four women and
one man—he does the gardening." He gave her a
crooked smile. "But, since I like my privacy, they are
all day help. None of them lives in the house."

A thrill of sensation skipped down Elizabeth's
spine. Without him spelling it out for her, by men-
tioning his preference for privacy, Lyon had reminded her of the night, the hours, they had spent
together in the library, alone, undisturbed.

Elizabeth felt her face grow warm, and hastened to
change the subject. "Is there a room I could use located close to the one you put Mitch into?"

"Several," he said, heading back in the direction
they had so recently covered. "Follow me."

The room Lyon ushered her into was located across
the corridor from the one in which he had installed

Mitch. Elizabeth paused in the doorway only long enough to give him a dry-as-dust look before entering the room.

"Will it do?" he asked, watching for a reaction—any reaction—from her.

Keeping her composure intact, her expression blank, Elizabeth glanced around her. Since the room was almost twice the size of her apartment bedroom, and contained its own bathroom, it would do.

While it was true that the room was not nearly as large, as carefully decorated, as plush as the master suite, Elizabeth didn't mind; at least she didn't have to share it with the master.

After completing her quick but encompassing perusal of her new quarters, Elizabeth turned to Lyon. "It will do," she said flatly. "Now, if you don't mind?" She arched an eyebrow. "I'd like to freshen up."

Lyon met her prodding look with one of his own. "I don't mind. There's the bathroom."

This time, Elizabeth's sigh held more the sound of a snort. "Didn't I just hear you say something about liking your privacy?"

"Yes," he responded mildly, innocently... too innocently. "Why?"

She gritted her teeth. "I like mine, too. So, will you please get out of *my* room?"

The sudden smile that tiptoed across his sensuously curved mouth did wild, frightening, and exquisitely exciting things to her central nervous system. "What are you afraid of, Elizabeth?" Lyon asked in a warm, soft, insinuating tone. "Me . . . or yourself?"

Feeling trapped, by him, and her own traitorous physical response to him, Elizabeth bared her teeth in a deceptively bright, defensive smile, and raked her mind for a suitable put-down.

"Why, myself, of course," she said sweetly. Then, just as his smile took on a tinge of self-satisfaction, she let him have it. "I certainly don't want to risk murdering you while Mitch is stuffing his face with pizza."

Lyon looked startled for a blink in time, then he tossed back his head and roared with laughter. He was still laughing as he retreated from the room.

"You win," he called back, obviously amused. "This round. I'll wait for you in the hallway."

Eight

The pizza was history. Hunt had long since left for home. Mitch was in bed. Elizabeth sat curled into a corner of the butter-soft leather sofa in the library, hands folded in her lap to keep from fidgeting, waiting for Lyon to broach the subject of the parameters of their necessary relationship.

"You're going to spoil him," she blurted out, no longer able to endure the silence, or the annoyance that had been eating at her ever since Lyon had secured his place in his son's affections by gifting Mitch with a sleek, black and silver ten-speed bicycle.

Lyon leveled a cool stare at her from where he sat—lounged—in a matching chair opposite the sofa. "So what?" he challenged. "I have nine years to make up." His lips tightened. "Nine years *you* robbed me of."

"Me...I!" Elizabeth sputtered, bolting upright. "How dare you accuse me? How dare you?"

"Dare?" Lyon growled back at her. "How dare I? You have got to be kidding. You're the one who dared to deny me the rights to my son."

"Rights? Rights!" she exploded. "We're back to rights again, are we?" She was shaking, outraged, furious. "You're the one who started this custody fight! You're the one ready to stoop to blackmail. Don't talk to me about rights. As far as I'm concerned, you have no rights!"

Lyon was no longer lounging, in fact, he had shot out of the chair to stand over her, his features rigid, his sapphire eyes glittering with angry sparks. "I must have been out of my mind to offer you anything other than what you deserve," he snarled. "Is there nothing inside of you but lies and deceit? What right did you have to run away ten years ago, denying me the right to my child?"

"Run away?" Elizabeth repeated, stunned by his audacity. "You...you...bastard! You drove me away!"

Her charge gave him momentary pause, and Elizabeth time to stand, backing him up, her chest heaving as she faced him with righteous indignation.

"Drove you away? How?" Lyon sneered. "By loving you more than my own life?"

"Loving me?" Elizabeth forced a harsh laugh. "Oh, sure. You loved me so much you married another woman."

Lyon blinked. "What does my marriage have to do with it? I didn't marry until years after you disappeared."

"But you did marry Leslie Broadworth," she persisted. "Didn't you?"

"Yes, I married Leslie. So what?" he said, shaking his head as if trying to clear his mind. "We were childhood friends, compatible. I convinced myself that friendship and compatibility were enough. I was wrong."

"About a lot of things," she gibed.

"Meaning?" he prompted, eyes narrowing.

"Oh, come on, Lyon," Elizabeth said in chiding tones. "I was young, and naive, but I wasn't stupid. I was there when your father came to our house, check in hand."

"My father? Check? What in hell are you talking about?" he demanded. "My father's dead."

"But he wasn't dead ten years ago." Elizabeth was losing her control, but she no longer cared. "He was very much alive then, very sure of the power of his money, very understanding, and very oily."

"You bitch." Lyon flexed his fingers, caught the reflexive action, and took another step back, away from her. "You dare dirty my father's name now, when he can't defend himself? Is there no end to your deceit?"

"Dare? Deceit? Again?" Elizabeth retaliated, incensed beyond reason or caring. "You want to talk about deceit? Okay, let's talk about deceit." She was crying and she didn't notice. Her voice strained, rising by degrees, she flung at him all the particulars of his humiliating rejection of her, verbally beating at him in fury, pain, emotional ravagement. She was so wound up, so overwrought, she didn't see the color draining from his face or the growing horror filling his eyes.

"No." His voice was raw, barely audible.

"Yes," Elizabeth spat, feeling spent, yet relieved at having at last purged the poison from her system. "Oh, the money paid the medical expenses for Mitch's birth and my schooling the following year," she admitted ungraciously. "But I hated it, every damn demeaning, *deceitful* dollar of it."

"Elizabeth..." Lyon stepped forward, reaching out for her with one trembling hand. "I can't believe...I didn't...my father couldn't..."

Elizabeth didn't comprehend, didn't want to understand whatever he was attempting to say. She cringed to avoid his groping hand and sidestepped away from him. "No, no," she muttered, moving toward the door. "Don't touch me. Don't you *dare* ever touch me again."

"Elizabeth, wait!"

She paused in the doorway to glance back at him. "I'm tired," she said, unmoved by the expression of bewilderment on his face. She gave him a cynical smile. "I'm afraid our little discussion about relationship parameters will have to be postponed until tomorrow." Exhausted, Elizabeth ran from the room, distractedly wondering if she was doomed to run from this same room, and Lyon, forever.

Elizabeth awoke after a restless night to clear blue skies, bright sunshine, and a blasting headache. By the time she had stumbled from the bed, to the shower, then back into the bedroom to dress, the pain in her head had subsided to a mild throb.

Seeking a reviving cup of coffee, with two aspirin on the side, she crossed the corridor, not really expecting to find Mitch in his room. If Elizabeth knew her son, and she did, he was outside, reveling in the sparkling sunshine of the late summer day.

After leaving the empty bedroom, Elizabeth headed for the stairs, determined to find the kitchen in this enormous pile of stone Lyon called home.

Lyon. Thinking of him brought a shiver to Elizabeth's flesh and a sigh to her lips. She would have to face him sooner or later. It may as well be sooner.

Instead of Lyon, she found Hunt cooling his heels in the great hall, waiting for her.

"Good morning," he greeted, crossing to meet her at the broad base of the staircase. "I've been designated a one-man reception committee."

"Oh?" Elizabeth murmured, trying for a casual air as she glanced around. "Why?"

Hunt's smile contained a wealth of understanding. "Lyon's not here. He had some business to attend to."

"I see," she said, experiencing a strange sensation of loss and regret.

"Are you hungry?"

"Not really, but I'd love some coffee," Elizabeth answered, glad for the diversion from her own odd reaction to the news of Lyon's absence.

"It's yours," Hunt promised, taking her arm to guide her through the hall to the dining room. "When you've finished," he said, filling a cup for her from a large silver urn set on a beautiful old sideboard, "I'll introduce you to the day help and give you a tour of the place."

"Thank you," Elizabeth responded, to the coffee and the offer. "Mitch?"

Hunt grinned. "Outside, riding his bike up and down the driveway. He's perfectly safe."

True to his word, as soon as Elizabeth declared herself finished, Hunt presented her to a pleasant middle-aged housekeeper-cook, three younger women, employed to keep the house clean, and a robust man who worked in the gardens, of which there were three.

The house was impressive, with sixteen bedrooms, ten bathrooms, and an assortment of other rooms, including kitchen, two dining rooms—one formal, one informal—living and sitting rooms, the library and a functional, state-of-the-art in-home office, complete with everything necessary to allow Lyon to stay on top of his vast business holdings.

"A person could get lost here," Elizabeth observed dryly as they strolled from the house in search of a breath of fresh air and Mitch.

"I know," Hunt agreed.

"So, why are you here?" she said bluntly. "Are you my guard dog?"

"Guard dog?" He gave her a startled look, then he laughed. "No, Elizabeth. At least not in the way you're obviously thinking." He smiled with gentle understanding. "It's simple, really. I hold the position of assistant to Lyon, and usually work out of his New York office. Last week, Lyon asked me to come down here." He shrugged. "But, I suppose, since Lyon had to leave, I am on guard duty until he gets back, but only in the sense of keeping you and Mitch safe here, at night." His eyes held a teasing gleam.

"Or would you prefer to be alone here, rattling around all forty-odd rooms?"

Elizabeth had to laugh. "Okay, Hunt, I got the point. You're not here to spy on me."

"Right." Hunt laughed with her. "Knowing Lyon as I do, I have the feeling I'll be gone, out of your hair and away, as soon as he gets back."

"And when do you think that might be?" Elizabeth held her breath, inwardly denying any sudden or avid interest in his reply, and telling herself she hoped he'd stay away a good long time, or at least until she returned to work.

"Who knows?" Hunt said, then changed the subject. "By the way, how is Chuck?"

"Fine," she answered, grimacing. "Although, at the moment, he's not particularly thrilled with my present situation."

"I can imagine," Hunt murmured, coming to an abrupt halt and placing a hand on her arm. "But if I could, I would tell Chuck exactly what I am about to tell you. And that is to be patient. Things will work out. Lyon is not really a hard man to get along with."

"Uh-huh," Elizabeth muttered, moving away. "But, if you don't mind, I'd rather not talk about Lyon."

"Whatever you say . . . except . . ."

"Except?" Elizabeth arched her brows, and smiled for the boy drawing closer to them.

"Mitch."

Elizabeth slanted a sharp glance at Hunt. "What about him?"

"Well, just look at him," Hunt said, grinning. "He is definitely Lyon's cub."

Lyon's cub. Elizabeth suppressed a shudder, while forced to acknowledge the accuracy of Hunt's description. Mitch was the living, breathing image of the younger, softer, more vulnerable Lyon she remembered.

Grinning from ear to ear, Mitch glided the bicycle to a smooth stop in front of her and Hunt. "Hey, Mom!" he crowed. "Isn't this place great?" Then, not waiting for an answer, he bubbled, "Did you know there's a swimming pool, tennis courts and even a miniature golf course?"

"No, I didn't," she began, only to fall silent when he rushed on.

"And we're gonna live here forever and ever. Dad told me so."

"Did he, indeed?" Elizabeth said, sliding a probing look at Hunt. "And when was this?"

"This morning, before he left," he answered, setting the bike going and zipping away again.

"Perpetual motion," Hunt observed dryly. "No doubt about it, Mitch *is* the Lyon's cub."

"What are you really trying to say, Hunt?" Elizabeth demanded, staring him straight in the eyes.

Hunt didn't blink as much as an eyelash. "Lyon is my friend as well as my employer, and I know him very well." His voice took on a note of urgency. "I've been watching them together since you arrived yesterday and, Elizabeth, please, be patient. Lyon needs Mitch, every bit as much as I believe Mitch needs his father. That's all I'm going to say. The subject's dropped."

Thanks a bunch, Elizabeth thought, battling a surge of resentment against Hunt for his unsolicited, patently bias, opinion. But, biased though it might be, she had to admit to the validity of a segment of his assessment.

Mitch did need his father.

Fool! Lyon berated himself for perhaps the one thousand and second time. He had been a blind, trusting, utter jackass of a fool all those years ago. To think, to know that his own father had betrayed him, his trust.

Elizabeth.

Pain, emotional, physical, wrapped around Lyon's tight chest. His father had betrayed him, and he, in turn, however innocently, had betrayed Elizabeth.

Was it any wonder she continued to defy and challenge him? Lyon reflected, cringing inside at the searing memory of his high-handed treatment of her. The real wonder was that she had acquiesced to his arrogant demand that she bring Mitch and come live with him.

But Elizabeth had acquiesced. Why? Why had she given in so easily? She could have made a fight of it in court, or even run, as he had expected she might.

But she had come to him.

Why?

Lyon clung to the hope hidden within that nagging *why* as fiercely as a drowning man clutching a slender life line. He had been clinging to the nebulous hope for nearly a week, ever since he had uncovered the carefully concealed facts proving the truth of her story.

Lyon was free to go home at any time. The personal investigation he had conducted to insure a measure of secrecy had been concluded almost three days ago. He had the facts, unpalatable as they were.

Elizabeth had spoken the truth; she had not run away from him, denying him his rights to his unborn child. She had been driven away...and by his own father.

Go home? Lyon shuddered. God, how could he face her? How could he look into her eyes, loving her as he now, finally, was willing to admit he did, and face the justifiable resentment of him in those soft brown depths?

Loving Elizabeth.

A feeling, a sensation too strong, too compelling to be identified as merely relief, washed over Lyon. Ten years, ten years of his life had been spent in denial of any and all emotions connected with Elizabeth. Inside, within the very fabric of his being, Lyon had erected a wall of bitterness, a shield behind which to hide from his own truth, the truth of his continuing love for Elizabeth.

Now the wall was down, the darkness of the shield removed, his needs, feelings, expectations exposed to the light of his love for her.

Standing at his office window, staring out over the most vital and exciting city in the world, Lyon felt an electrical shock sizzle through his mind, his body, unrelated to the bustling metropolis.

He *was* free! He was scared, damned scared, but he was finally free.

Spinning away from the window, Lyon strode for the door. He was going home, because he was free; free to apologize to Elizabeth, for his father and himself; free to tell her of his feelings; free to ask her, plead with her, beg her, on his knees if necessary, to stay with him.

The golden light of sundown was blessing the earth when Lyon brought the silver sports car to a stop in the curve in the driveway in front of his house.

Quiet, serenity, permeated the landscape. Lyon sat still for a moment, drawing strength of purpose from the air of tranquillity. During the long drive home, he had given thought to selling the house—his father's house—to begin anew, relocate to somewhere, anywhere, away from the scene of his ill-considered actions. But now, absorbing the sense of peace surrounding him, Lyon rejected the idea.

The house was not his to sell. Regardless of the outcome of his entreaty to Elizabeth, he would not, could not, sell the property. The house, the grounds, were not his to dispose of. They were his son's inheritance.

A movement caught Lyon's attention, and he raised his eyes to the front of the house just as Mitch stepped through the doorway. His son. An unprecedented thrill shot through Lyon, propelling him from the car.

"Hi...Dad," Mitch called in a soft, uncertain-little-boy tone of voice.

Lyon felt a thump in his chest at the hesitant, unsure way Mitch raised his hand in greeting. Obeying sudden impulse, Lyon held his arms out in welcome as he strode to the steps.

"Hi, yourself," he responded in a voice even he recognized as tight with emotion.

There was an instant of continued uncertainty, then a radiant smile broke over Mitch's solemn face and, with a joyous whoop, he launched his lanky young body off the top step and into his father's embrace.

Holding his son close to his heart instilled within Lyon the most wondrous sensation he had ever experienced. While strands of awe, gratitude and undiluted delight wound themselves into a ribbon of pure love around Lyon's heart, a warm rush of cleansing tears filmed his eyes. Through the film, he saw Elizabeth emerge from the darkened interior of the great hall.

Elizabeth looked every bit as unsure, as uncertain as had her son.

"Hello," he said, despairing the crack of emotion in his voice, the pain in his heart, as he stared into her rigidly composed face.

"Hello." Elizabeth's voice was as strained as his own, but also cool and withdrawn.

"Elizabeth . . . I . . ." he began, not sure where to begin.

"Geez, Dad," Mitch piped in, giving Lyon a hard squeeze before stepping back to look up, jewel-bright eyes wide and shiny, at him. "I was gettin' scared you wouldn't get back before Mom left."

Every living cell inside Lyon seemed to freeze into a solid mass of fear. "Left?" he said, slicing a stark look at Elizabeth. "Where are you going?"

"Back to work."

Lyon was hard put to keep his pent-up breath from whooshing from his throat. "When?" he asked, trying to appear casual as he draped one arm around Mitch's shoulders, drawing the boy with him as he mounted the steps to the door, and Elizabeth.

"The day after tomorrow," she answered, backing into the hall as he advanced.

"Can't you put it—" he started.

"No," she said, giving one sharp, determined shake of her head. "I won't."

"Elizabeth, we must talk." Though he was careful to keep his voice soft, as natural sounding as possible, for Mitch's benefit, his urgency came through.

"Relationship parameters?" she said in tones of weary resignation.

"No... well, yes... but, not exactly," Lyon of the usually smooth response, fumbled. "I... er..."

"Hey, Dad!" Mitch cried, slipping out from under Lyon's arm to grab hold of his hand and tug on it with endearing eagerness. "Come see what I found to show you!"

Lyon felt torn between the urgency to begin his campaign to convince Elizabeth that they belonged together, and an equally important need to establish a foundation of affectionate companionship with his son.

"Elizabeth?" he murmured, resisting the stronger tug on his hand, his heart.

"Go with him," she said, shrugging, as if to make her disinterest crystal-clear to him. "Our discussion has waited this long, it'll keep until after dinner."

Fighting off an encroaching sense of pending defeat, Lyon stared at her indecisively for a second, then

capitulated to the obvious excitement motivating his
son.

Mitch danced ahead of Lyon up the staircase, along
the corridor, into his bedroom, and directly to a card-
board box, upended, contents littering the carpet.

"What have we here?" Lyon inquired, perusing the
assortment of papers and articles scattered about.
"Your secret treasures?"

"Nah," Mitch said, flashing a sly grin. "This is all
Mom's stuff."

Lyon's interest was immediately caught. "Your
Mother's?" he murmured, dropping to one knee for
a closer look. "Does she know you have this in here?"

"Well, no...but, all my report cards and honor roll
certificates and that stuff were in there," Mitch explained in an apologetic rush. "And...I—I thought
you, er...like...might want to see them."

Lyon melted, and relented. "I would," he said,
dropping fully to the floor.

Lyon spotted the vaguely familiar-looking jewel-
er's box midway between honor roll certificates and
sports citations. "Well, what's this?" he asked, taking pains to appear casual as he picked up the case.

"Oh, that's only a broken old bracelet of Mom's,"
Mitch said, turning away to paw through some papers.

Breathing slowly in an effort to control a gathering
sensation of tingling expectation, Lyon pried the lid of

the case apart with trembling fingers. Inside the case, the clasp broken but still gleaming, lay the gold chain bracelet he had given to Elizabeth in celebration of her eighteenth birthday.

She had kept it, hidden away, all these years. Hope surged with wild abandon inside Lyon. Maybe it meant nothing at all. Then again, dear God, maybe it meant everything there could be.

Dinner was the longest meal Lyon had ever had the pleasure to endure. His pleasure was derived from the innocent enthusiasm of his son. His endurance was in direct relation to the bracelet burning a hole of promise in the pocket of his pants.

Finally—finally—the house was quiet. The day help had gone their separate ways. Hunt had been dispatched back to New York. Mitch was in bed. Elizabeth was once again curled into the corner of the sofa in the library. Lyon was in a state of anticipatory terror.

"Let's get this over with," Elizabeth instructed, nudging him out of his state into action.

"I'm sorry."

"What?" She frowned.

He drew a deep breath. "I said, I'm sorry."

"Okay." She eyed him warily. "For what?"

"Everything." Lyon exhaled harshly. "Oh, God, Elizabeth, you will never know, words cannot ex-

press, how very sorry I am for all the pain, humiliation, and damned pure hell I have put you through."
He raked a hand through his hair. "I know the truth now about what my father did to you, and to your family, but, as God is my witness, Elizabeth, I never as much as suspected before you told me last week."

Comprehension chased the look of wariness from her face, replacing it with relief and...what? Compassion? Pity? For herself? Lyon wondered. Or for him? God! He didn't want her pity. He wanted her love!

"Elizabeth, listen to me—" he began urgently.

"May I go now?" she asked, cutting him off.

"Go?" Lyon could barely speak; he couldn't breathe at all. "Go...where?"

"Anywhere," she answered softly, bluntly. "Away from here, and you."

Lyon felt his chest muscles contract, as if in protective reaction to the killing thrust of a naked blade. He closed his eyes and, for one instant, truly wished to die. The talisman tucked in his pocket transmitted a silent message to him to not only live, but fight.

"Yes, you may go now, if that's what you want," he said, sliding from the chair to the floor. "But first, please, hear me out," he pleaded, breaking through a cautioning whisper from pride. On his knees, he crossed the carpeted space separating them.

"Lyon?" Confusion tinged with alarm shadowed her beautiful eyes. "What are you doing?"

"Anything, everything I can think of to keep you here, with me." Her hands were clasped in her lap. Cradling them in his own, Lyon raised them to his lips. "Elizabeth, will you listen, hear me out?"

She was trembling. So was he. Her eyes were overbright from a fine mist. So were his.

"Lyon, I can't believe...what are you saying?" she asked in a broken outcry that swelled his heart with hope.

"I love you, Elizabeth." His voice was raw, serrated with pain. "I loved you ten years ago. I loved you all through those ten years while I was hating you. I loved the girl you were, but I love you now, so much more, more than my own life, even more than my own son."

"Lyon. Oh, Lyon...I..." She was crying openly now, sobbing, unable to continue.

Thrusting his shaking fingers into his pocket, Lyon withdrew the bracelet. "I found this," he said in a voice every bit as shaky as his hands. "Will you wear it for me again?" he pleaded, fastening it around her wrist. "Love me, again?"

"I never stopped loving you," she cried, bending to kiss the fingers circling her wrist. "I wanted to. I prayed for the strength to hate you. But, as deeply as I loved the son you gave me, I have always loved you."

"Oh, sweet Lord, Elizabeth!" Sheer, unadulterated exhilaration singing through him, Lyon clasped her by the waist and drew her down onto the floor beside him, in almost the exact spot they had shared before the fireplace weeks ago.

"Lyon!" Laughing, crying, Elizabeth circled her arms around his neck, and hung on. "What are you doing?"

"Loving you," he said, unashamed of the tears spiking his eyelashes. "In all the ways I know how." His eyes gleamed with a happy, teasing light. "Geez," he mimicked their son. "That okay with you, Mom?"

A sensuous smile curved her lips. "Geez, Dad, I thought you'd never ask."

There, in front of a crackling fire, cool air washing over their passion-flushed bodies, Elizabeth and Lyon made sweet, hot, soul-consuming love to one another.

Murmuring soft words of love, praise, gratitude, Lyon kissed, caressed, and claimed as his own, every inch of Elizabeth's body, drawing first sighs, then moans, then ecstatic cries from her parted lips.

In her turn, Elizabeth explored, stroked, laved every inch of Lyon's length, drawing first grunts, then groans, then exultant shouts from his arched throat.

When, at last, quivering with desire, they blended, mouths, bodies and spirits, into one perfectly attuned entity, their union was sealed with the promise of a lifetime of love.

Dawn was painting the horizon a blushing pink when, momentarily satiated, Lyon raised himself up over Elizabeth and stared with unabashed adoration into her sleepy brown eyes.

"Live with me."

"I will."

"Love me."

"I do."

"Marry me."

"Of course."

There was an instant of utter stillness. Then the silence of dawn was broken by the sound of their combined bursts of unfettered, joyous laughter.

* * * * *

SILHOUETTE® *Desire*®

MYSTERY MATES!

Six sexy Bachelors explosively pair with six sultry Bachelorettes to find the Valentine's surprise of a lifetime.

Get to know the mysterious men who breeze into the lives of these unsuspecting women. Slowly uncover—as the heroines themselves must do—the missing pieces of the puzzle that add up to hot, *hot* heroes! You begin by knowing nothing about these enigmatic men, but soon you'll know *everything*....

Heat up your winter with:

#763 THE COWBOY by Cait London

#764 THE STRANGER by Ryanne Corey

#765 THE RESCUER by Peggy Moreland

#766 THE WANDERER by Beverly Barton

#767 THE COP by Karen Leabo

#768 THE BACHELOR by Raye Morgan

Mystery Mates—coming in February from Silhouette Desire.
Because you never know who you'll meet....

SDMM

Take 4 bestselling love stories FREE

Plus get a FREE surprise gift!

SILHOUETTE® Desire®

MAN OF THE MONTH: 1993

They're tough, they're sexy...
and they know how to get the
job done....
Caution: They're

MEN AT WORK

Blue collar... white collar ... these men are working overtime
to earn your love.

January:	Businessman Lyon Cantrell in Joan Hohl's LYON'S CUB
February:	Landscaper-turned-child-saver David Coronado in Raye Morgan's THE BACHELOR
March:	Woodworker Will Lang in Jackie Merritt's TENNESSEE WALTZ
April:	Contractor Jake Hatcher in Dixie Browning's HAZARDS OF THE HEART (her 50th Silhouette Book)
May:	Workaholic Cooper Maitland in Jennifer Greene's QUICKSAND
June:	Wheeler-dealer Tyler Tremaine in Barbara Boswell's TRIPLE TREAT

And that's just your first six months' pay! Let these men make
a direct deposit into your heart. MEN AT WORK... only from
Silhouette Desire!

MOM93J